AF481783

GUS

BY
KEN FOSTER

Copyright © 2024 by Ken Foster

All rights reserved.
No portion of this book may be reproduced in any form without
written permission from the publisher or author except as
permitted by U.S. copyright law.

DEDICATION

"To the Dog, no one wanted, including me at times, but we had each other's Back! Gus really was my dog. He was hit by a Truck. He died on April 19th, 2024, He was a royal Pain, and he is Missed dearly every day! Like I said in the Book HAPPY HUNTING BUDDY

PROLOGUE:

She took her last breath Three minutes ago! I looked into our sons' faces and saw exactly what I was feeling: Loss, Despair, almost horror! She and the boys were my world! How do I bury my heart? My soul died with her last breath, so how can I go on to live an ordinary life? I want so badly to crawl up in bed with her and die! How do I bury my heart?

Greg, my oldest son, looks stunned like he didn't think it was possible for her to go and that she would somehow find a way to pull through! Teresa had that way about her. She not only had a zest for life, she almost demanded it to her will!

Chip, my middle son, had that same shocked look like she was playing a game and would jump up to hug them and say got ya but she would never hug her babies again! How do I bury my heart?

Ernie, my youngest, just cried, and then his brothers went to his side, holding one another, Each one keeping the other from falling into the same abyss that I'm free-falling into! I needed to go to them, but I couldn't move; I know I'm a selfish old bastard and only worried about myself, and I love those boys dearly, but I can only think of my loss until I realize they must be devastated!

My legs feel like rubber, and I can't breathe! I have to sit! Maybe I'm in shock myself. I don't know; my mind drifts back to a few months ago when she was giving me the TALK, the one where she laid everything out for me!

First, you take care of my Boys, even the little Black one, Gus! Gus is the Lil puppy she rescued from the shelter and has been nothing but a royal pain in the butt since! Chewing on everything, peeing in my boots, whining when she leaves! There is Mutual Dislike between us, and if he had boots, I might repay the Lil fart!

Half Rottweiler and half hound, he lets his nose get him into all kinds of trouble, from getting into the trash to chasing any animal within a three-mile radius.

Teresa told me that financially, we were in good shape. The house, vehicles, and the small farm we bought a few years ago were all paid for. Ernie's tuition might need supplementing, but most of his was covered by his scholastic scholarship.

She also told me, no, she demanded that I love again! We hardly ever fought, but that really pissed me off! I was scared, and all I wanted was for her to fight and pull through this, knowing all along she was fighting a lost cause; she was just as scared, and all she wanted was for her loved ones to be taken care of!

She looked up at me with those beautiful green eyes and chewed her bottom lip like she always does when she is about to tell me something she knows I won't like, then say's Sweetheart, you will do this. You will fall in love again, and you have my blessing! I said I don't want your damn Blessing; I want my Wife Then I regretted saying it. Knowing all that did was make her feel guilty for something she had no control over!

Coming back to reality, to a new, darker, colder reality, one without my ying, To the Here and Now, I guess. I know my boys need me, so I force my legs to stiffen and walk to them, grabbing them all in a hug that we all need! Looking at my beautiful wife one last time! She looks so peaceful, and with the pain finally gone, you can see her native heritage even with her hair gone because of her treatments, treatments she didn't want but my selfish ass made her take to get just one more month, one more second one more warm beautiful smile.

For the next couple of years, I was lost in drinking and fighting with anyone who looked at me sideways, taking my pain and trying to make it theirs! But it was me that really paid, yeah there were a few asshats bullies that got their ass whipped, but after two years of drinking, fighting, and getting thrown in jail, my friends turned against me, I was about to lose my job, and I just couldn't stand myself anymore when Greg my oldest said one sentence that made me wake up " Mom would be ashamed of you "" I was Pissed but deep down I knew it was true because I was ashamed of myself! He was right, and I knew it, so I slowed way down on drinking and stopped going out!

Greg started coming over when his business would allow him, and we would take fishing and hunting trips from time to time. Sometimes, Chip and Ernie straggled home, and we would all hit the woods for some well-earned family time! Chip was in the Air Force as an F-35 Pilot, and Ernie was an associate physics professor at MIT.

Our talks always found their way back to their mom, and like them, I missed her so much, but spending time with the boys when they were in town helped. One day, one step, then one breath. After that, I would go home to Gus to one screwed up one hundred pounds of attitude; I know it sounds like I hate him, but I don't; I just don't like the Damn dog!

TABLE OF CONTENTS

CHAPTER ONE:
THE FALL

Even after Two years of Teresa's Death, I can't stop thinking or dreaming about her! They really did bury a part of me with her, and I can't see how I can ever recover! I'm really just punching life's time clock, waiting for my final paycheck, which, with my health going downhill, shouldn't be long! High Blood pressure, Type II Diabetes, Asthma, then add all of my brain farts that kept my doctor shaking his head! There isn't a part of my body that doesn't hurt now, including my Soul especially my soul. My sons are the only refuge from doing something stupid!

I work More than I should at Distillery to help keep my mind off that black anniversary and even took a third shift to keep away from the prayer squad, but it Doesn't keep the sorrow away! If my coworkers saw the tears, they didn't call me out on it!

I stopped on the way home to put flowers on my lady's grave and give her updates on the kids and myself and to cuss at that damn dog she loved so much I had taken two weeks' vacation, so I had plenty of time to lay around and talk to her, but I knew I needed to get to the farm and feed the animals, including the black hell-yuan!

We (I still say we instead of I) have two good Quarter Horses, Two Jackasses, four Beefalo heifers, and a Beefalo bull that is starting to make some money breeding!

I'm not sure why I'm writing this or if anyone will ever read it, and if they do, they damn sure won't believe it!!! But it is all true Scout's honor!

My Name is Jack Welch, and I'm writing this so someone will know what happened, at least from my perspective!

So, I get home and feed the animals, then head to the house; I grab the leash and bottle of bud lite then ask the asshat if he wants to go for a walk, so he slowly walks over like always does when he has done something bad and knows he is in trouble then stands there for me to attach the leash and open the door before I find his indiscretions! We head out toward the backlot! Walking along, enjoying a beautiful fall morning! Gus pulls me to the old sinkhole that the previous owners used as a dump and burned garbage. You know, the things you would get hung for today, and in my opinion, rightfully so! I'm no environmentalist, but I'm smart enough to know we only have one planet, and we are killing it. Sucking up resources, Over populating it, and sooner or later, Earth, God, or Mother Nature will say enough is enough and something big will happen like it's done before. But enough of the ramblings of an old broken man.

Gus must smell deer droppings or something because he is pulling me hard to the sinkhole and then stops to smell the ground! Thinking it is a good time to drink my beer, I turn it up for a good long pull, enjoying the burn on the back of my throat when I hear a yelp and a pull from the leash and then nothing but air because the ground opened up and swallowed us both! I land face first in dirt and garbage, then Bam, a bottle hits me in the back of the head, and then everything goes dark! I woke up a few minutes later, according to my watch anyway, sitting up spitting dirt and cussing Gus. I reach for my mini-Maglite. I carry on my belt for working Nights and turn it on, shining it around the hole we have fallen in! I wasn't sure what I was looking at, but it seemed to be some sort of tunnel! Checking my body to make sure everything is still working, I feel something hard under my right leg, and I shine the light at it to discover it is just an old metal fence post! I use it to help me stand up, and there before me is a smiling Gus looking like he had done something stupendous and waiting for his treat, damn dog!! I go to kick dirt at him as my other foot slips, and I bust my ass. Yeah,

Karma really is a bitch; sorry, I'm trying to slow down on the cussing!

Then I see light coming from one end of the tunnel. Curious, I get up and walk over to take a look, using the fencepost as a walking stick to help out my sore knee. My jaw dropped when I saw where the light was coming from! It looked like water was flowing straight up vertically through a big round window, and the light was shining from the sun on the other side! It was beautiful and scary as hell at the same time, standing about twelve feet tall and round! If people were with me, they would be screaming at me, telling me not to touch it!

Yes, yes, I had to touch it, but before I got there to where I could touch it, I felt something brush my legs, and I saw Gus dive through to the other side. Then I saw what looked like his shadow run down a hill! Barking at some poor unsuspecting animal, and as much as I dislike that damn dog, scared but not knowing if I'll see Hobbits or a Rabbit with a Hat, I knew I had to keep a promise to my wife and get the black ball of fur, so I walked through!

CHAPTER TWO:
DIFFERENT SEASONS/DIFFERENT TIME

Armed only with a fencepost, a pocket knife, and a bad attitude, I walked out into what looked like a spring day! Woods all around, I was standing on a small ledge facing south, or I thought, but I wasn't sure because there should have been the Western Kentucky Parkway, but there was only one big wooded valley!

About twenty feet down the hill was what I think was a game trail, but it was pretty large, and what was really throwing me off was the typography looked like it was close to as it should have been minus the WK parkway

Looking to the left, I see Gus running around the bend of the game trail, barking loudly and being an obnoxious damn dog! So off I go half sliding and a half walking down the hill to the trail I last saw that black fartbox go! Reaching the trail While walking and hollering for Gus, I get a few feet when I see Gus running back my way! Smiling and thinking he was finally starting to listen when I saw this huge black bear right on his heels, so I did the manly thing and started running back up the hill toward the tunnel!

Forrest Gump would have been proud!

I was thinking, Run, Forrest, Run! If that bear were going to bite, then it would have been my Butt because this old man was moving! I was passed by the black furball (Dog not Bear) about halfway up! I dig in a bit harder, and as I hit the ledge, I grab the fencepost and turn to swing, but there was nothing there! I looked back down the hill, and the bear was walking back the way it came, uninterested, which kind of pissed me off, so I roared at him. Then he stopped, turned, stood up on two legs, and roared back! That thing had to be ten feet tall and well over six hundred pounds, so I did the brave thing and scampered my little Unhappy ass back through the portal, grabbing Gus's leash as I went. I took one last look before I walked through and saw trees budding on what seemed to be a warm spring day. But how was it even possible that It was spring here and almost fall there? I know the date because that day is ingrained in my scythe: September 28th. The day two years ago, my better half died, so how were leaves budding here and turning there, and where was the Western Kentucky Parkway?

Tying The Hellhound up on a tree root, I made my way up to my barn to find my extension ladder, which made getting that fine animal out a little easier! After a shower and feeding everyone, including myself, I was bushed and hit the bed, but for some reason, I couldn't sleep thinking about what Gus had gotten us into, so I called Greg, My oldest, and asked him if he could take a few days off for a little exploring and if he didn't mind to bring one of his drones, not sure he believed me when I told him about my day, but he agreed to meet me in the morning!

CHAPTER THREE:
GREG

After hanging up my phone, I laid back down, gazing up at my ceiling fan as it spun its unbalanced blades. Being a little OCD, it took his mind off worrying about his dad for a bit! Looking down at the foot of the bed, he saw the balancing tab lying there, so he grabbed it and took it to the Kitchen, where he had some superglue in a drawer! Sixty seconds later, the fan spun like a dream, so his mind drifted back to his dad!

All three brothers had the deepest respect for their father! He may act like a brainless dork and at times had his share of brainfarts (As his dad called them), but all three boys knew the man probably better than he knew himself! They saw him stop in a snowstorm to help an old lady change her tire so she could make it home safely! Greg even saw his dad take out a loan to help a friend, knowing he would have to pay the loan off!

Sometimes, his dad was too good a man for his own good, but that was the type of man Greg strived to be, and that was the reason all three brothers were so worried about their father when their mom died! The world needed more Men like Jack Welch, not less, so Greg grabbed his cell phone and called his brothers!

Chip leaned over to look at his cell and saw it was his brother and slid off Captain Ali. ''Shitstorm,'' Shoptowh said sorry, babe, this may be important! Laying naked on his stomach Shitstorm said it better be and reached over and pinched his butt hard then said and that was for leaving me hanging!

Chip watched her slip off the bed and head to the bathroom for a shower Thinking to himself how in the hell did I get so Lucky?

He answered the phone! Brother, this better be good because I have the Hottest female officer in the Air Force naked in my shower!

After ten minutes on the phone, Chip said I'll put in three weeks' leave and be there as soon as possible after my shower, so you better call Ernie before his dorky ass goes to bed! Then, hung up and rushed to the shower!

Ernie was working out a mathematical problem on the old blackboard when his earphones switched from Pantera to Greg! Fourteen minutes later, Ernie said let me make a couple of phone calls and book a flight, and I'll be home as soon as I can! After he hung up he looked at the Equation thought to himself I will solve you one day!

CHAPTER FOUR:
BACK IN THE HOLE

Getting up sore was usual for me but I had to almost roll out of bed the next morning! I dressed for the woods (Meaning Camo) fed the barnyard animals, Fixed Gus and me some eggs, sausage, and biscuits, then grabbed the backpack I used for camping, canteen, and shotgun, strapped my Sig 1911 45 Calibor and holster to my side, thinking of the bear I grabbed my Shotgun with a few Deer slugs! Looking around to see if there was anything else I needed, I saw a bottle of Knob Creek Bourbon on my bar, and with a smile, I put it in the side pocket of my backpack. Then, taking Gus, we headed out to the front porch to wait for Greg!

It looked like a gorgeous morning with just a little chill in the air; we hadn't even gotten our first frost yet! Teresa loved this time of year, but my old bones hated cold weather, and I knew what was coming after fall, so even though I loved the fall colors, it put a damper on my mood a bit! Greg showed up a few minutes later and climbed out of his Land Rover; seeing the wax seal of my Knob Creek sticking out of my pack, he snickered and said are you sure you weren't nipping on that yesterday at the sinkhole?

No, smartass, I wasn't, but I did drink half of a beer before devil dog pulled me in the hole, damn dog!

Greg chuckled and said one day, you are going to miss ole Gus and bent over to scratch his neck; all I could do was huff but he didn't know how right he was! At the sinkhole, I carried Gus down and tied him to the tree root again, then went back up the ladder for my pack! It took a few minutes to get to the portal, and Greg stood there with the same bewildered look I had yesterday! Greg said that it looked like the Portal from Stargate but without the chevrons. Then, remembering the movie, I had to agree!

Greg is a smart guy, maybe not the smartest in the family. That moniker had to go to Ernie, but Greg started a tech company inventing a few gadgets to use on cell phones and Tablets! He was making a name for himself in the tech world! Since Teresa was gone, I often relied on Greg's opinion on anything to do with both Technology and finances; really, all three of my kids are uncannily smart, but I'll get into that later on

Gus was at Greg's side when we all stepped through the portal! Not knowing what we would see when we went through it, I was relieved to see the same landscape as before! Greg bent down and unhooked Gus's leash and told him to stay with us and not run off! The mutt listened and walked right beside him; sometimes, I hate that damn dog! We walked for about an hour or so with woods on both sides. When we started downhill, an opening in the trees appeared! The view was spectacular; we were about one hundred feet up above the Valley floor, and we could see where the trail ended down below us into an open field just above a river with the cleanest water I had ever seen!

I heard a gasp and turned to see Greg take his caps off the scope of his Garand rifle and point it across the river. Hoping it wasn't the bear again, I went into my pack for my spotters' scope, and there across the river was a herd of buffalo! It had to be seventy head! Greg said I thought this game trail was big, and now I see why, but we haven't had Buffalo in Kentucky in over two hundred years, not in these numbers anyway!

I told him back then they used to travel up to Salt River and all the salt licks around Bullitt County! Salt mining was Kentucky's first industry. We walked down to the river to see how deep and cold it was! it was spring here, so it was still a little chilly, and I said no skinny dipping today. With the look on Greg's face, I Had to snicker! The river was so clear you could see fish everywhere, and as I sat down by a tree on the bank, I heard a whoosh and an arrow stuck in a tree where I was a moment ago.

Looking up startled, I grabbed my Shotgun that was leaning against the tree with now two arrows sticking in it, so I then grabbing my pack and dove behind the fallen tree Greg was sitting on, planting my face in the dirt! it seems I'm becoming a connoisseur of dirt lately, and this dirt tasted a bit sweeter. It's strange how your mind works when under stress sometimes!

As Greg fell back behind the tree, he asked what have you gotten us into this time, I smiled and said, "Gus did it. "Speaking of Gus, where the hell is he I asked, and we both peeked over the tree and saw four men, well, Indians, I guess because all four had Mohawks war paint and wore some sort of buckskin pants with no shirts! Three was at the edge of the woods, and a big ugly one was out in the open about forty yards out! Looking at the one on the far left, I saw a black shadow standing there and pointed it out to Greg, so he yells Gus, don't just stand there, bite his ass! The brave had an arrow notched and just starting to put tension on the bow when he heard a growl behind him! Keeping the bow pointing in the same direction, he slowly turned his head to the side to see almost One hundred pounds of fur, muscle, and teeth staring back at him; he dropped the bow and made one step before Gus latched on to his butt! There was a loud scream and Greg and I both smiled until I heard a war cry and looked at the ugly guy that decided to charge!

He was faster than I expected, and he was on me in no time, so I dropped my shotgun as he launched himself in the air, tomahawk in hand. I ducked slightly, bringing my arms up. I tried using his momentum against him. I grabbed his neck with my left hand and placed my right hand on his stomach while pushing up. I was hoping to flip him into the river behind us! I didn't hear a splash, but I did hear a thunk. I took a quick peek over the side to see him laid out on a large rock on the edge of the river with his neck at an odd angle "damn, my bad, "was all I could think of saying at the time, feeling bad for taking a life I tried to distract my mind from thinking of the here and now by looking at Gus as he worked his head back and forth while still having a mouth full of butt as the poor guy was still running we heard a rip and yell as Gus stood there with buckskin blood and bits of the Indians Butt! Slowly, Gus turned to look at the other two braves, and that was all it took as they took off north toward the Ohio River just as fast as they could go! Gus finally earned his keep.

We both sat down for a minute to calm ourselves when I caught sight of Gus walking to the edge of the woods with his tail wagging curious, I got up and walked over to see what he was up to and saw Four women tied together! They were tied with their hands in front and then to a rope that was tied to an old oak tree.

Three looked to be native Americans and the other had blond hair! I pulled my tactical knife out of my sheath and started forward, but I looked up before I got there to see all Four were terrified, so I slowed down and talked in a calm voice that I wouldn't hurt them when the blond started talking to them in a different language!

The First Lady was the Blond, About 19 years old. She said the name her parents gave her was Sara, but her Choctaw name was Nita. The second was a short girl about 17. Sehoy was her name, and that sounded vaguely familiar but I couldn't remember from when! Opa was next, a 19 to 20-year-old, and the last took my breath away. When I looked into her eyes, all I saw was Teresa! The face was a little different! The nose was a bit wider and her hair a little darker, but she was biting her bottom lip, and her Beautiful green eyes were exactly the same! Greg was even lost for words! Her name was Aponi, meaning Butterfly Which was Ironic because my heart was so full of them, I thought my chest might explode.

CHAPTER FIVE:
FOUR LITTLE INDIAN GIRLS

They were all dressed in the same way, which led me to believe they were taken from the same place! I figured the Blond had been with them for a while, well, since she Spoke their Language. Communication was tough because she spoke an ancient form of English with a lot of Thee and Thou's but we found out she was kidnapped from her family's farm about ten years ago off the coast of South Carolina by the Muscogee tribe, what the Whites called Creek Indians then sold to the Choctaw where she was married and had a son. Her husband was wounded when she was taken by the Mohawk but she thought he was still alive! Nine people were captured in the raid and taken north from their Village that sat on the banks of the Big Muddy River. I think the Mississippi, somewhere in Alabama maybe Mississippi! Four women here and five young braves!

I asked where the boys were, and then she said they were at the Cave waiting to be sold to the Big Grays! I had so many questions, but the first was what cave and where. Then she said Giant cave two days walk that way, pointing south! Greg said Mammoth Cave, which in our time is a state park! Sara went on to say the Grays were Demons that flew through the sky on metal horses and were bigger than any man she had seen! To distract her from going into a panic, I changed the subject and asked her if she knew what year it was! She thought for a few minutes and said I am not entirely sure, but it may be the year of our lord Seventeen, Fourteen, or Fifteen. As I looked at Greg, my head started to hurt wondering how that was even possible!

Greg and I started setting up camp for the night while talking about the Situation! I looked up, and Gus was right under Aponi's feet, just like he had been with Teresas, so I yelled at him to go get us a couple of rabbits for dinner. He looked at Greg when Greg shook his head yes, then the meathead took off wagging his tail. Twenty minutes later, he came back with two good-sized rabbits! I always knew Gus was smart because Teresa worked with him as a pup when she was home sick from her treatments. His problem is that he is hardheaded! I have always heard you have to show them who the Alpha is, but after two years of showing him who his boss Is, well, you get the picture!

The girls grabbed the rabbits and Aponi came over to me with her hand out! Lost in her Smile, my Heart hammering in my chest, Greg broke my revelry, saying she wants your Knife! I told her to be very careful that it was sharp. She just smiled that beautiful smile, and they all headed for the river, Gus right behind her. Happy and lucky!

While they were gone, Greg and I talked over what we should do, and we both decided we should help them and see if we could rescue the Braves! I told Greg that my dark world finally has shown a little light, but I would love for things to slow down a bit! At that moment, I had a vision in my mind of laying in the sun on that riverbank, a cooler full of beer, headphones on, listening to some good blues while having a fishing pole laying on my chest as I dozed off and hoping I didn't get a bite but knowing that wouldn't happen at least for a while so We planned to head back to the house in the morning to refit and get the horses & Mules and I really wanted a bit more firepower!

CHAPTER SIX:
THE BEAR

After dinner, the sun was just about to set when Gus started growling. I was trying to see where he was looking when I noticed a big black shape come out of the woods a little over 200 yards away. He was walking slowly and sniffing the Air! Damn, he smells the blood from the Rabbits! Kicking myself for not burying the remains! I knew better than that! I bent over and picked up Greg's Garand rifle and asked, do you mind? Go for it was the answer.

I looked again and he was just about seventy-five yards away and stopped looking in our direction and I started thinking he might just go away when Gus took off circling it biting and snapping then came running back which must have pissed the bear off because he started at us again Damn dog!

So, I shouldered the weapon and pulled the trigger. A click was all I heard! Looking at the gun, I quickly found the safety, released it, and started raising it again, but the bear was just a few feet away, standing on two legs. Gus pounced on one leg, biting and growing as I was trying to back up and shoot without taking good aim! I shot as I was falling backward, hitting my butt. I was still scrambling back as the bear fell between my open legs just about a half-inch from a part of my anatomy, I hold very dear to my heart!

I laid back thinking you are really making a good impression on Aponi, and why that mattered, I didn't know!

After my heart slowed down enough for me to speak, I said how about we put him in the cold river until morning to clean? We can tie him to a tree to keep him from floating off, and the river will keep him cool and the meat from spoiling. It took every one of us to roll him down the bank and into the crisp, clean water and tie him off! I was bushed, It's Hell getting old!

Greg and I both had a five-man tent we carried in our backpacks along with a sleeping bag and emergency blankets, so I gave my tent to the ladies just using the lite weight blanket and laid down by the fire! I was out in less than a minute!

CHAPTER SEVEN:
BACK TO THE FUTURE

I woke a little after dawn and I opened my eyes to find an older Indian brave sitting cross-legged less than three feet from me with a tomahawk in his lap! There were three other braves around him! I tried to scoot back but someone was behind me! There spooning up against me was Aponi and the other three right behind her wrapped up in my sleeping bag! I said in a low voice. Sara, Wakie wakie, the old man laughed and said I like you, White man! Surprised I said you speak English. Some he said then I heard Opa say Apisa (Later found out it meant Father) and looked to see her run to him! He said so, you like sleeping with four women at once then laughed when I stuttered a no, hoping he was just ribbing me!

He introduced himself as Koi or Panther in Choctaw! I told him about what happened with the Mohawks and Bear and Greg, and I planned to be back here by tomorrow morning to help rescue the braves held captured. Then he volunteered to skin the bear and put the mohawk in his final resting place! I handed him four plastic trash bags for bear meat and I would imagine he wondered what they were made of!

So, Greg and I broke camp and headed to the house! I called my older brother as soon as I got a signal to have him meet us at the barn! Lee was an old hippy, A Vietnam vet who loved his pot and anything Indian! He had an archeological degree in something or another, and other than Ernie, is one of the Smartest men I Know. He has burned more brain cells than I'll ever acquire, and he has burned a lot!

Greg went up to saddle the horses and jackasses. I went ahead and got on the bobcat skid steer to dig us a ramp down to the tunnel to get the horses down! I then went into the house and restocked on food and water also getting my AR 15 and a box of birdshot and deer slugs for the shotgun!

I walked out as Lee pulled up, and I offered a beer and told him the story while he unloaded his Quarter horse and mule, then waited for a smart-ass comment and was very surprised when I didn't get one! He had a serious look on his face when he asked if this was true, and I'm still not sure if you haven't been eating the other kind of mushrooms or not, but you need to be very careful not to screw up your timeline! You could have already screwed up by just killing the bear, who is to say the bear was supposed to kill another animal that was supposed to be killed, or even if it's the bear that Daniel Boone was supposed to kill? I said well, that would be a very old bear because that isn't going to happen for another 50 years or so, but I get your drift! He asked if that Bear was the other bear's Daddy.

He was right we had to be very careful!

The next morning, we walked the horses and mules down the ramp, through the portal, and down the hill, where we mounted up and headed to the river! About halfway there Greg and I heard Lee say hollieeeshit I thought you sniffed one too many fermenters but you ain't lying This place is Gorgeous Lee may act like a Tommy Chong wannabe, but he actually has a brilliant mind, and I started wondering, with him, my wife, and kids, how I got left out of the IQ raffle.

CHAPTER EIGHT:
BACK TO THE PAST

A big smile spread across Lee's face as he said hmmm, This would make for a great growing season, and I knew what he had in mind when I said TIMELINE. Then I heard him grumble," Stick in the Mud"! We pulled into the camp, and Koi had the bear processed, but still working on its hide, I gave him Veronica, one of the mules (Named after an old Asshat Girlfriend), so one of the braves could take Sehoy. Sara and most of the bear meat home to their Village!

After tears, hugs, and thank yous, they headed southeast toward Alabama/ Mississippi the Choctaw was a mound-building tribe right off the banks of the Mississippi River and Lee told a story that Sehoy was from the Muskogean tribe and a pretty important person she would one day be married to Jean Baptiste Marchland from Louisiana and have a son who would grow to be a fierce warrior and one day become a Choctaw chief called Red Shoes! Red Shoes actually ignited the Choctaw Civil War! So, you see how important being careful really is, Lee replied, referring to the timeline!

We loaded up with Aponi right behind me and Greg and Opa on one of the other horses. Oh, and good ole Gus running right beside Aponi. Koi rode Sally Lees's supply Mule, the other three braves running along, one in front, the other two behind us! I saw the looks Greg and Opa were giving each other and I have to admit I felt a little excited about it! I had been trying to get Greg to slow down and find someone for a while (I wanted Grandkids to Spoil), but the business he was building was his baby!

He dated Here and there but nothing took! They always wanted more than he was willing to give! I just hope Koi didn't take exception to some White man making googly eyes at his daughter!

CHAPTER NINE:
BEAUTIFUL WORLD

I had a hard time believing how Gorgeous Everything was before man had trashed it! I still remember the old commercials about littering where an Indian was standing by a highway with trash everywhere and he had a tear running down his face! If the Indians only knew what was ahead of them, the Broken promises, The Trail of Tears, and the trashing of their Mother Earth, they would rise and wipe us all out, and who could blame them? Looking at this pristine landscape with crystal clear rivers and lakes. animals grazing without fear is enough to make me want to stay!

I know life would be harder, with no A/C and no University of Kentucky sports (Which may be a blessing in itself at times). Oh yeah, I still hate Christian Laettner! But life could be so good here!

One thing is for sure in that I would need to find a way to secure that portal but little did I know that portal would be the last of my worries.

A little after five pm, we were about a mile away from the cave, and everyone started making camp! Koi, Greg, and I snuck off to scout the caves and to see what we were up against! The caves were surrounded by woods but there were a few open spots! We crawled to the edge of the ridge overlooking a small Valley and in one of those clearing were four silver objects sitting on the ground! They looked like Jet Ski with two large glowing runners down each side! I bet those were the flying metal Horses that Sara was talking about! Some sort of Anti-Gravity or Hoverbike! there looked to be about fifteen people in the cave wearing collars of some sort, with three Indian guards that looked as frightened as the slaves and four large gray beings that would even make Predator pee his pants. A plan started to inch its way through my noggin.

At dawn, Greg and I would try to disable their bikes making as much noise as possible to get the grays away from the others while the others snuck in and took the three guards down and got the slaves!

Oh, the best-laid plans of mice and men! I'm not sure anyone will ever refer to me as a tactical genius, but it sounded good at the time. I just wished I knew about the personal shields the grays had and the anti-theft shields on the bikes! Who Knew?

So, I had my shotgun loaded with birdshot, then deer slug. birdshot deer slug I also had my right pocket full of birdshot and my left full of deer slugs in my tactical pants. Greg had my AR15 four thirty round clips with 5.56 NATO rounds, and we both had our handguns. Surely that was enough. Well, the Gods must have said, don't call me Shirley because it would take everything we had! Early the next morning, I led the way because I was older and wiser with more life experiences. When we got close to the bikes, I began to regret destroying them because they looked astounding, with screens, buttons, and knobs everywhere. NASA would have a field day with them! I started to reach for it.

I when heard Greg say I wouldn't I looked at him and with a smile that said don't tell me anything because I'm the dad and I know what I'm doing then, as I touched it, I heard a pop and a big electric jolt as I flew through the air landing on my back I sit up, shake my head to get the cobwebs out and said Great googly moggggally I think I had smoke coming out of my ears! Greg started laughing and said I told ya, so at that point, I looked at the cave as all four grays piled out and were heading our way! They were Sixty yards away and walking fast in our direction! I had to wait until they were close for my shotgun to do any damage, but Greg started firing right away. When he hit, there would be a blue flash but nothing else! The First one was one of the smaller ones that only stood about 8 and a half feet tall and all four had some sort of armor on with a personal shield because Greg bullets were just blinking off with a blue flash then after about eleven rounds his armor blinked off and Greg next three rounds took him down! So, when the next guy, well, he really wasn't a guy, but when he was close, I hit him with the Birdshot, then racked the gun and hit him with the deer slug, and his armor winked out and blew a chuck of his chest out! Thinking this might not be too bad when the next ugly sob stepped over him, he had to be close to ten feet tall! With a shriek and an evil look on his face, he started to run at me, so I racked my shotgun and shot. Then, by that time, he was diving for me, and we rolled! I had my knife out in my left hand and 1911 in my right and emptied all nine 45-caliber rounds point-blank! He had both hands around my throat and my lungs were screaming for air as I started to black out I saw this black flash hit him as sweet blackness took hold not sure how long I was out but I could only be a second or two because I look up and see Gus on top of the gray bastard and giving him hell so I roll up to one knee while grabbing my shotgun and racking a shell one-handed then yelled to Gus to heel! He backed off, and I shot, then racked and shot! Right after his shield winked out, I shot a Deer slug, and then he was down, so I turned to see how Greg was doing! The last one grabbed Greg when I ran out of ammo for the shotgun, so I yelled for Gus and saw the three of them topple over in a heap of elbows and black legs. Then I heard a snap! Nothing scares a parent more than seeing their kids in dire trouble! Running over to see how Greg was doing, I saw Gus with the gray neck in his mouth and his black tail wagging, and Greg smiling! Seeing they were ok, I walked over to the biggest one, not sure he was dead, but he was, and as I kneeled down for a closer look when his Arm armor jumped off his Arm and onto mine, Reforming to fit my arm then a second later I felt a sting in the middle of my arm and passed out! When I woke up Greg was standing over me with one on his arm also! I said I guess it is a bit late to warn you not to get close! He smiled and said Just a Tad.

CHAPTER TEN:
TAKE A RIDE

Greg gave me a hand up with a big grin on his face! It usually takes me a minute or two to get up because of my achy knees, ankles, and back, but for some reason, I didn't feel what I was expecting (Pain). Hell, I felt great! my body felt loose, strong, and agile and my mind felt sharp! Greg told me to look at the bikes, and when I did, I suddenly knew how to start and operate them. Not only that, there were formulas and specs! I'm not a stupid man, but I barely graduated high school because of Algebra; now I understand baseline physics!

We walked over and picked up the other two Arm Bands off the other two greys to keep them from hurting anyone else when Aponi and Koi started walking up the hill talking! I understood every word she said so I asked her when she learned English with a strange look on her face, she said she was speaking in The Western Muskogean language as she came closer the armband in my hand flew out of my hand and stuck to her right arm Gus Yelped and whined as I rushed over to catch her because I knew what was coming then she passed out! Greg grabbed his other armband with both hands as Koi got close, but it was to no avail. It latched on the same as the others. I guess it was looking for a host! Once They woke up, I could see the wonder in their eyes when they looked at the bikes! I helped Aponi to her feet, and we walked over to look at the bikes with excitement. Then she smiled and said let's go! I grinned and yelled down to Lee that we would be right back. Then we all hopped on a bike and took off!

Flying about a thousand feet above the treetops, we were really scooting when I thought about falling off, but then my mind reassured me that the Forcefield would keep us on! I'm not sure how fast we were moving, but heading east, we hit the Atlantic

Ocean in about twenty minutes! We turned around and headed back! I thought we might have a hard time finding where we started but the screen turned on with a language, I didn't understand then changed to English and asked our destination first line said Previous Destination the second said New Destination the third said Manual guidance so I hit previous and it took over and set us back in the same spot it came from! As we were landing, I was wondering how its guidance system worked because there wasn't a GPS satellite in orbit at this timeline. When the answer came, it was a good thing we were back on the ground, or I would have wrecked! My mind said the Ship handles all navigation of the grave Sleds while planet side!

Ship! What ship, I asked myself, and who the hell is talking to my mind, and then I knew! I saw an image of the ship, and it was big and Beautiful in orbit behind one of Mars's moons, Phobos! My god, I'm going nuts. I had no idea what any of the names of the moons were. Hell, I didn't even know there were two, and now my head was full of scary-ass information! I need a drink and I was awfully glad I brought the bottle of Knob Creek but the question was, was the bottle big enough then I knew that answer also, "Damn It".

SECTION TWO

CHAPTER ELEVEN:
KEEP YOUR FRIENDS CLOSE

I guess everyone has heard the term Ignorance is Bliss. Well, that was always my guideline! I knew just enough to get by, sometimes just enough to get me into trouble but not enough to get me out, and that is where Teresa came in! She was my Ying, and I was her yang. What I lacked, she had my back on, and what she lacked, I had hers!

We were perfect for each other. we just fit! There wasn't another woman alive that could turn my head and that is what pissed me off when she told me I would love again and it was okay by her and I thought she was crazy but now I Look at Aponi and how I'm now drawn to her the same way I was to Teresa Then I wondered Do I have a real Future? Before I was just living one day at a time until I found Teresa again in the afterlife now for the first time in a long time, I'm actually looking forward to seeing what tomorrow might bring After Burying the grays and gathering up their weapons and Armor, we Used the Bikes to move the camp by the river to the caves to give everyone shelter until we could figure out what to do! I pulled everyone off to the side that could speak English and told them everything I knew and Aponi translated for the rest!

I knew how the portals worked and why the greys, better known as the Enoc's, used them to not only teleport to Earth but also to teleport back in time to the Seventeen Hundreds!

They did It to get slaves, mainly because the resistance would be almost non-existent in this timeframe, and they took thousands and thousands to different worlds! The docile ones they sold as slaves, the more militant they sold to zoos, or if they could be turned, they would join their military, and some destroyed! They loved the younger slaves because they had a higher success rate at turning!

They didn't make as many credits from the Military as the others, but it was a good avenue for taking most of the more militant while still making a profit, and the Enocs were profit-driven. They also had a side hustle in mining! I looked up at shocked faces as the information spilled out of me as dispassionately as If were reading a book! The others with armbands already knew some of this, but like my mind, your answers didn't come until you asked yourself the right questions, and I could tell by their facial expressions they were now getting answers they didn't like! I saw a smile every so often but mostly frowns and even Aponi broke down and cried and I moved over and hugged her until the sobbing slowed then stopped not sure I wanted to ask her what her mind was telling her but found out later she had a younger brother taken years before and never knew what happened until now! It seems the Enocs are a brutal species! They wouldn't take too many from any one time period or too many from any one race to keep from wiping out whole civilizations! They learned from their mistakes because they almost made the Aztecs completely extinct, and many of those they took they had to Destroy because they were too Militant! So, they tried getting slaves that would have died by either shipwreck or wars, but if they were short on time, they would just grab a few here or there like now. If there were missing people on earth then they were probably either snatched as slaves or were someone's decedent that was taken decades before! Wasn't there a whole Roman Legion that disappeared without any trace? This may not be one hundred percent accurate but the chances were there to be true!

CHAPTER TWELVE:
GOOD NEWS

Not all of the information I gave them was bad! I told them about the original owner of the armband I now wore and how the armband also acted like keys! Whatever he owned was now the property of the new armband owner. Then I could tell each owner, asking themselves questions and confirming by nodding! Greg lucked out he was now a minor lord and second in command of the ship, a fairly wealthy aristocrat with two enoc wives, which I found funny, but he didn't for some odd reason.

Aponi was the ship's navigator and pilot. She was also wealthy! They all received a good portion of the profits from the Slave trade and Mining! Koi was the new weapons officer and Security chief! They all asked in unison WHAT SHIP, but I didn't have to say a word. They received their answer. At least the people with the Armbands and all looked at me and smiled! Well, I did end up answering for Lee and the others without the armbands I told them about being the new owner of a new Star Carrier that was parked behind one of Mars's moons, and then I dove headfirst into the research that I've done through the armbands that they were really living sentient beings that needed a living host They also injected Tiny nanites into the hosts Bloodstream Where they would replicate until a certain number then stop until more was needed! They would also travel to a certain part of the brain and build a receiver to communicate with the Armband and then to the ship's computer system. There was a process of removing them if they chose to, but a replacement host would be needed! No experience was necessary because the armband was like a living AI and would train as it saw fit it also was linked to the ships' computer and operating systems for instant analysis and data. All the operator needed to do was ask the right questions at the right time. The Armband could be turned off or reprogrammed by the host if wanted or needed!

I then went to each individual and asked point-blank if they wanted to keep it or give up a chance of a lifetime! Greg was first and the one that scared me the most because he had so much to give up! He turned and walked to the entrance of the cave, looking out after a few minutes he came back and stuck out his hand and said I'm IN Aponi and Koi didn't need money or power. All they wanted was for their village to be safe, but when I asked her, she walked up to me, looked at me with those beautiful eyes, and said Cute white man needs my help. Then tiptoed and gave me our first kiss! I melted and lost my train of thought! I looked at Greg to see what his reaction would be but saw a big smile Koi said he wouldn't kiss the scraggly old white man, but he had to think about it because he didn't want anyone or anything controlling his thoughts. I couldn't blame him, but in my mind, the possibility of the good far outweighed the bad. After dinner, he walked out of the cave, climbed to the top of the ridge, and sat down looking out over the valley.

Getting the collars off the slaves was pretty easy; it turns out there were three buttons on the front that had a code that had to punch in in the Wrong sequence, a small explosive would detonate, severing the spinal cord and killing the user instantly. We asked the slaves if they wanted to join us, but most just wanted to go home to their loved ones. Even though we did get four volunteers, three young women and a young brave all Choctaw, which made communication a bit easier for them at least!

CHAPTER THIRTEEN:
HEADING HOME

Early the next morning we sent out two hunting parties to give those that were going home enough food until they got there. Two braves went south with bows and arrows, and Greg, Opa, and Gus went east! They both came back with one carrying a doe and the other a Wild Turkey! We tried to cook the juices out of it to make jerky the other they packed with as much salt as we could find. By noon Koi walked back into the cave and told me he didn't want the armband but he wanted to accompany us on our journey, that he believed he could help us in other ways so I asked him to hold off on taking it off until I had a replacement and it may be a few days to a week and he agreed but Lee stepped up and said he would like to take it so I asked how and was told that the new host needed to cut his arm and then press a four button sequence on the armband to release it from the user! With that done it jumped from Koi's arm to Lee's.

Lee woke up with Gus standing over him, so Gus did a Gus thing and licked him twice before Lee could push him off and sit up! Lee said there was no telling where that tongue had been, so Gus did a gus thing bent over and licked himself, then looked at Lee with a smile! I told you that dog was both smart and an asshole (Sorry for the language) So, I looked at Lee and knew he was popping off questions left and right. As his smile got wider, I asked Well, and he said, to hell with Chat GPT. This thing has all the answers I've been looking for! I said yeah, I can't wait to get an armband on Ernie.

CHAPTER FOURTEEN: GETTING EVERYONE WHERE THEY WANTED

I gave Gayle the last jackass to those going home, hoping it wouldn't change the timeline too much, and they took off about noon. A few minutes later, Lee and two of the young females took off for our old camp! I was wondering about the wisdom of this as I had visions of them passing a joint around while a war party snuck upon them! Greg did send Gus with them to keep an eye on them, but I wasn't sure who would keep an eye on whom. They made it five hours and probably three joints later because they were all smiles and hungry as hell, even Gus the damn dog!

After Lee had left, I didn't think about Koi not having an armband and had to give permission for the bike to be ridden by Koi, so! While Lee was on his way, Greg and I rode our hoverbikes up, parked them in front of the portal, and walked through.

We found Chip and Earnie on the front porch, Chip sipping a beer and Earnie drinking a Big Red cream soda! We sat on the porch for over an hour telling them all that happened to us the last few days, and I could tell Chip wasn't buying it, but Earnie was all in spitting out equations and theories! Even the armbands couldn't shake Chip's doubts!

Standing there before the portal, Earnie was feverishly writing away in his notebook while Chip could catch flies with his mouth open. It is true he said more of a question than a statement! Shall we? I asked, pointing to the portal when Chip asked what about the other one. Is the portal going to the ship? I told him I wanted everyone going at once. I said we all have a stake in this, and all would discover it together, and then I walked through the portal, followed by Chip, then Greg. We had to go back for Earnie! It wasn't that he was scared. He was writing everything down with this mesmerizing look on his face!

More wonders to come, I said as Greg grabbed one arm and I the other and pulled him through! He noticed the seasonal change right away and started writing again. Then he noticed the bikes and almost broke his neck while getting to them! I climbed on, and Earnie got on behind me, then Greg and Chip on the other! Before we left, I had to talk to them and see what their thoughts were, so I asked, we now have control of a Time Portal, Hoverbikes, and a star carrier, so now what? Chip said we are going to need some help! Scientists then Security. Ernie said we really could bring Earth out of the dark ages and think of the knowledge we could all gain, but we must be careful, or we could lose it all! He was right. I could see some Big Corporations or governments trying to steal everything from us, so we would need to think hard about how we could protect the Portal, the Bikes, and the Carrier! It was starting to get late in the morning, but I wanted to take them for a little joy ride before heading to camp!

I have always been a proud papa because Teresa and I raised three good, smart young men! They all brought something different to the table, and my heart was busting to have them all here sharing this adventure.

After Greg & Chip did a couple of barrel rolls, we settled down at the camp and got everyone moving toward the portals! We had a little problem getting the horses up the hill and through the portal. They knew what was coming and didn't like it but with a little coaxing and a bag of carrots later we got them through and bedded down in the barn!

I was thinking we might want to wait until morning to go through the other portal, but the look on everyone's faces told me they couldn't wait anymore; Christmas was about to come early!

It was just like the other portal, but instead of traveling through time, we would be traveling through Millions of miles of space in an instant! We were standing there, and everyone wanted me to go first because it was my ship when Gus broke through and leaped through the portal Damn Dog!

CHAPTER FIFTEEN:
THROUGH THE RABBIT HOLE

So, there I go chasing the damn mutt once again, thinking he may yet be the death of me when we come through in a room in what looked to be a med bay! I moved Gus off to the side so others would have room to come through when they came one at a time! Things were getting a bit crowded when the last came through, and we heard a voice saying that decontamination had been initiated after a few seconds! After a body scan, a door opened, and the voice said Decontamination complete, but as soon as Lee walked out the door, the voice asked him to wait for the auto doctor. After everyone else was cleared there were two patients waiting for the Auto Doctor! Lee and one of the young girls rode with Lee, but I didn't know her name yet! She was told she was pregnant and due in eight months and ten Earth days! I looked at Lee, and he said Don't look at me. She is Cute but way too young for me! I knew he was telling the truth, but I had to give him a little ribbing. That's what little brothers are for!

Lee was told he had a spot on his left lung and given a Shot in the right arm through a wall dispensary and told to come back to any of the eight med bays within seven earth days for another body scan to make sure the nanites repaired all the damage the cancer was causing!

Everyone waited outside the Med Bay for us to come out, and I was just about to ask for a map of the ship when a voice sounded! Excuse me, Lord. This is the ship's Artificial Intelligence, and it has been my duty to run the ship in your absence! Since you are the new owner of the Eye of Torrox, would you like to continue in this manner? The Eye of Torrox, I asked; then he said that was the Name of the Ship that Lord Elos had given it, but it could be changed with the new ownership.

I told him I would think of a new name and asked how I could refer to him when he is needed! He said that it is also at my discretion! I told him AI would work until a Suitable name could be given, then asked if he had any preference, and he said No! I then told him/her/IT to assign Quarters to everyone and try to get them close to the Bridge.

I then told everyone to settle in and grab a bite to eat from one of the mess halls and then meet me on the bridge in two hours, that we had plans to make! While I made my way to the closest mess hall, I wondered what I would do with Gus and his bathroom breaks. Then I thought we could install an extra shower that had running water when he tripped a sensor and would flush down a drain, then trip another sensor to shut the water off when he walked out! The AI saw what I had in mind and drew up the plans, then told me a Construction Robot was on its way to my cabin and would start construction, and completion should be within two hours! I guess he doesn't get Coffee breaks! I walked into the mess hall that was closest to the bridge! We could call it the Officer's mess anyway. I was wondering who would be cooking and if there were any supplies we could eat! It was a big room, it looked big enough for close to a hundred men at least! Everyone was sitting and eating Burgers and fries! I was about to ask Greg who was cooking when I got the answer in my mind! I thought to myself, this is going to take some time to get used to! Anyway, there was a food replicator that could produce any food on Earth! Lord Elos First tried to go into the future to steal his slaves, so he recorded each year's digital history from the Internet for two hundred years until he saw there was a better chance of getting caught, and that is when he decided to go back and steal from the past! I thought fast and told the AI to lock down any data from two thousand twenty-six on unless I gave the okay! Knowing the future could open a can of worms I'm not ready for; hell, what's happening now is still blowing my mind!

I gobbled down a bowl of chili and washed it down with a Bud Lite, wondering if the nanites would let me fart or if they would fix it where the gases would dissipate hay. I get strange thoughts when I'm left alone, and my mind told me that it was up to me that I could turn them off or force them to bypass that particular body function, which I did!

CHAPTER SIXTEEN:
ROOM FOR A KING

As I was headed to the bridge, I thought I might want to look at my quarters. Greg and Chip were with me, so we walked in to see! I was expecting a small bed, desk, and small bathroom but I guess the Enocs didn't do anything small! My house could almost fit in there! Everything was in a bright white! It was nice and looked to be easy to keep clean, but it was in need of some color, which was a task for another time! The bed looked like a double queen! I asked the AI if there was a closet Safe and small armory for my personal use and slid the door open for me.

On the left hung three sets of body armor! Elo's was eight and a half to ten feet tall and I was five foot nine on a good day! I asked the AI to have them removed and repurposed if possible then he told me everyone was scanned and they would have three sets plus bodysuits delivered to each person's quarters within the hour.

If any other clothing was needed, each person with an armband just needed to visualize what was wanted and approve it for the replicator to start! I knew some people would have been in hog heaven! At the end of the closet was a door leading to the safe and armory! Our eyes grew wide, looking at all the weapons. Didn't know what they were, but they looked very deadly that's when Alfred gave us a good rundown on all their capabilities and restrictions!

On the right on the floor were stacks of gold bars that looked to be about forty or so, then two stacks of what I first thought was silver but turned out to be worth in some markets more valuable than Gold. It was Palladium! Greg said the last he checked, Gold was worth twenty-four hundred and fifty dollars a troy ounce, and there were at least one hundred twenty-two bars! I asked the AI what the current market value was and his answer was only 522 million five hundred sixty-four thousand Eight hundred dollars and thirty-eight cents as of the close of business yesterday with the Gold and Palladium Combined! I mumbled. I guess I can take early retirement from the Distillery.

On the left side of the closet was a glass container with pinkish liquid inside were 32 armbands! Greg asked the AI what they were for, and he said they were new and dormant! They needed to be activated before use, and once activated, they would need a host with in thirty-six hours and would last until their death. Then I asked what we needed to do if more was needed, and he said the Med Doc would clone as needed! Chip said he would like to have one and thought Earnie would also! I asked the AI what needed to be done for that to happen, and he told me I needed to assign permissions and duties. I said Greg would continue as Second and Chip Chief Military, but he would need to wait until Obligation was up so resigned his commission with the Air Force, and Earnie would be Chief Science Officer If both agreed! Greg and I would need to pull double duty until we could all close down our other responsibilities! I asked the AI to activate an armband for everyone who wanted one but Chip and let me know when they were ready!

We walked to the bridge to find everyone already there; I guess curiosity had gotten the better of all of us, and we weren't disappointed! I don't think a design team from Rolls Royce could have made it any more luxurious. There were two levels with six stations on the top level and four on the bottom! The room was almost oval-shaped, with a screen covering three-quarters of the room! I looked at Greg and asked if we could get some University of Kentucky football games on that thing. I said jokingly, and then my mind received a yes answer! The seating looked to be designed for giants, Which I guess they were, so I asked the AI if the seats could be replaced.

He said right away. Then I asked what each station was assigned to, so he went through the arrangements, including the Lord's Station!

Then we asked for a Conference room to conduct meetings, and behind us, a door swooshed open, and we all piled in. It looked like the table could hold twelve, so eleven should fit just fine; hell, the chairs were so big they could almost fit two!

CHAPTER SEVENTEEN:
WHAT'S NEXT?

I started the meeting a bit early since everyone was already here! I asked What is next? Should this ship be a Warship, A ship of science or Exploration, or all three? We could just run the ship with just the personnel we have here, but to me, that's Selfish! Just think of how this ship could uplift Earth! When the AI told me the Armbands were completed and everyone on board wanted one except Chip and Koi, I told everyone to line up behind Ernie! The whole process took about thirty minutes, with the person behind catching the one in front and me catching the last.

Let me tell everyone what I have in mind for everyone! Greg, I want you as my Second, as I said before! Chip, first, while you are here, I need an inventory of all Air and Spacecraft we have on this ship and what their capabilities are! We are going to need Help. I want you to Recruit Military personnel for Air, Space, and Elite Ground Forces! This includes the Air Force, Space Force, Navy, Army Marines, and even everyone wiping boy the Coast Guard! I first want the people you trust! Not your drinking buddies but people who are both capable and whom you can trust with your life! The AI is capable of Flying this ship, but we need to bring the people of Earth up to where we are in a space fairing world, and that won't be easy! The only time our country came together was when we had a common enemy; otherwise, the liberals hate the Republicans, and the Republicans hate everyone, including themselves! Meanwhile, we have puppet masters manipulating everyone while we are busy fighting each other, at least in our neck of the woods! I would love to take this ship and turn its technology over, but we can't because all that would do is the most powerful nation would start WWIII the rich war machine would end with all the power and riches, and the weak would become weaker, sorry

I'll get off my soapbox now and I saw Aponi look under the table to see if I were on a box which made me smile.

AI, I would like to rename you Alfred! He asked if that is in reference to The Batman Alfred. Yes, it is Alfred! Well, should I adjust my Voice Modulation to speak with an English Accent? That is up to you, also Alfred. Can you close the Portals from here? Which set of portals would you like to Close? Which set? Wait, how many sets are there?

Two onto a Habitat on the planet you call Mars, Four on the planet Earth, and Two on a Habitat on Earth's Moon! Did Lord Elo Control all of them? No, just the two in the United States and the Four with the Habitats on Mars and Earth's Moon! Are any of the Habitats Inhabited? Yes, Fourteen in both. Twelve Slaves and two Enoc's on both!

Well, who is ready for another rescue mission? Everyone raised their hands! We only need five people! Aponi said I'm going with you, and then Koi said he would like to go. I shook my head yes to Both, then asked Koi to find One Brave he could trust, and then I asked Chip to go! Greg, I need you and Earnie to dig in and learn as much about the ship and its capabilities as possible, and both of you need to think of people we can trust who we may need!

Also, Alfred, could you fit everyone with the Armbands with their own battle suits? Ernie, look into the suits themselves and see if you can boost their shields and offensive capabilities. Oh, and Alfred, give Greg, Chip Ernie, Lee, Koi, and Aponi full access to everything that is available to both this ship and all equipment owned by me! Done was his response!

Alfred sent me a message stating that the Information that I wanted Chip To pull for me was on my Slate tablet on my Desk! I asked where my desk was, and he said it was in my office. A door behind me slid open, and I walked in and saw a big desk console. A clear tablet lit up Shows a list of all aircraft and spacecraft available and their use!

Something was nagging me at the back of my mind like I was missing something pretty important, and then it hit me! Alfred, you said Lord Elos controlled Six portals. Who controls the other two?

They are still being used as of today by a pirating race called the Walls!

One portal is set up and operational in a warehouse in Northeastern Bacolod city in the Philippines, and the other is submerged in a wall freighter just southwest in the Sulu Sea! I asked what were they doing there. What was their endgame? He said I'm not sure what you are asking lord that is when I said I am not a lord I'm just a man and this goes for everyone here you can call me Jack except my boys and you better call me dad or I'm whipping your ass I said with a smile. Alfred said Jack, I think you are asking what the Walls are doing in the Philippines. Is that correct? I shook my head yes.

Their operation started August 30, Philippine time, at three thirty am when they kidnapped twenty-seven family members of twenty sugar cane plantation owners that produce Muscovado sugar, a molasses type of sugar. And so far, they have accumulated six thousand tons of muscovado and eleven hundred and three Filipinos. The Sugar is very rare in their sector and very expensive to obtain!

Ernie, I need you to get with Alfred and go over the schematics of those battle suits like right now! He said, on it, lord jack, Dad laughing, so I looked at Greg and asked are all my kid's smartasses? He grinned and said the apple didn't fall far!

Chip, I need to postpone our mine rescue and send you back early to do some recruiting. We are going to need some special ops people: Seals, PJs, and a couple of Space Force Guardians if possible. Next, I asked Alfred. I'm sorry to pull you away, but do we have a communication device Chip can take with him so he can contact us here? He said yes, lord jack, Dad, we have a few different types! I just shook my head even the AI was a smartass. He said don't worry about pulling me away because I'm very good at multi-tasking! I can do billions of functions in a millisecond! I said that sounded like bragging; then he came back with ''Aint no hill for a high stepper, ''giving his best, Woody Harrelson. Can you give him a device, please? Yes, daddy jack lord, sir, it is being fabricated right now, and a service bot will deliver shortly. I looked at Chip and said once you get planet side, contact Alfred and have him send you a list of recently retired special ops personnel that you can interview, then pick the best you can find that still has his head on straight, then send that list to Alfred to do a deep dive into his life from birth until now! Doing everything from scythe evals to sleep apnea. I want people we can trust, so I'll give the final interview on the planet side. I then looked at Lee and asked if you knew any good corporate lawyers or patent Attorneys. He said a lady I dated a few years ago had a daughter who passed her bar exam a couple of years ago, and I heard she went into corporate law! Her mom had the biggest, but before he could say, I jumped in and asked if he trusted her. He said yes, that she was a really good girl and sharp as a tack. I said good, you are coming with me! I then told Alfred he needed to fabricate at least a hundred of the communication devices. He said they would be finished in fourteen minutes if I wanted to wait. While I was waiting, Ernie called from one of the ship's labs and said he figured out why the shields didn't last very long on the Battle suits! It was because the battery pack they used was pretty old and weak, and he and Greg were looking at fission reactors. The smallest one they found was the size of a cooler, but he thought it could be downsized to fit on a battle suit. Their design was genius, but the software was broad and unfocused. I would like to bring in a few people on the helmet, and with both a few hardware changes on servos on the suit and software changes on the display on the helmets, we think we can increase speed, the strength of the suit, also increase the vision and accuracy with power left over making these suits a Force multiplier by itself.

I said that's good, but I'll need those suits within a week, so how long before you can test the fission reactor? Greg said with the simple design of the reactor and the fabricators on this ship, probably   four hours with Alfred's help also that would at least give you unlimited shields, most likely up to a thermal nuclear event That should Be enough. I laughed. Get started as soon as possible. Then I looked at Aponi and asked her to talk to our Choctaw friends and find a job suitable to their abilities. She nodded and then said yes, cute white man, lord sir, Dad Jack! I shook my head and then turned to Chip, who was seeing Aponi for the first time, almost in tears, when I leaned in. Half hugged him and whispered no bud, it is not her then, guided him and Lee out the door, telling everyone we were heading planet side, each one of us grabbing the com device as we headed to the portal!

CHAPTER EIGHTEEN: RETIREMENT AINT WHAT IT USED TO BE

It was dark when we got back, so we brought all the hoverbikes into the barn and covered them with an old Army tarp that Lee gave me years ago. Then, while he loaded up his horse and mule, I drove Chip to the Air Force Reserve base in Louisville, where he said he could grab a ride back to Wright Patterson! When he picked up his duffle bag, I told him to let me know when he had at least three prospects, and I would ride up and interview them! He said he already had one, but she didn't know it yet, and I thought, Oh Boy, I would love to be a fly on that wall to see that conversation. I started to say something but bit my tongue. Some lessons a kid is better off learning themselves! When it comes to women, the old saying you can lead a horse to water but can't make them drink doesn't even come close! I learned a long time ago that Women are smarter than men, and we are not just in the same league but not in the same Universe! I told Teresa once that Women should be leading the planet, and she gave me one of those sly, sexy smiles and said how do You know we aren't I just turned and said Yes, Ma'am but knowing that wasn't so because if it were true this world wouldn't be so screwed up and with fewer Wars.

On the drive home, I told myself that I really needed to tell the boys how their mother and I met and resigned myself to do so as soon as we were all together again.

I got home about one am and let Gus run for a bit before bed, so I grabbed a couple of beers and headed to the front porch swing with some BB King playing on my old Stereo. I really needed a bit of a break with everything going on. I was a damn near overwhelmed, so I sat there looking at the stars, wondering where Aponi, Greg, and Ernie were, when someone walked up behind me and grabbed my shoulder, making me jump out of the swing and almost making me need a change of clothes! I cocked my arm back, ready to swing, and saw Aponi standing there behind the swing! With my heart hammering a thousand beats a second, I asked what she was doing here, and then she said she finished her interviews and got everyone settled and wanted to be with me! Looking into those green eyes and that beautiful smile, I knew I would never be able to say no to her! I had to look away because looking at her made my heart ache for Teresa and made me feel guilty for wanting more when my wife hadn't been gone but for two years! I really needed to talk to my boys to make sure they would be okay! I took her hand, sat her on the swing beside me, then opened the other beer and handed it to her. She took a little sip and wrinkled her forehead like Teresa used to do when she was concentrating! Thinking she didn't like it, I said if you don't like it, I'll get you something else when she stuck her hand out to stop me, she turned the bottle up and killed it. Then, while handing me back the empty bottle, she then took mine and killed it! I said I'm going to go throw these in the trash and put a lock on the refrigerator door! She smiled and said okay, Jack. When I came back out, she had the swing almost touching the roof, and she was giggling like a two-year-old! I had to laugh, and I knew I was going to fall hard for that beautiful lady.

I got her one of Teresa's old nightgowns, something thick and plaid, something about as non-sexy as I could; then took her to the guest bathroom and showed her how the water worked and put a little bubble bath in the tub for her and handed her some bath soap as I turned to hand her the soap her deerskin dress hit the floor then she gracefully walked into the tub and I not so gracefully pole-vaulted out of the bathroom sweating like a pig! After her bath, I put her in Ernie's old room, tucked her in, and went to bed! The next morning, I woke with her spooning up behind my back and Gus right behind her, so I leaned over, tapping on his shoulder and pointing at the door. He woke up and saw me pointing toward the door. He slid off the bed, pouting as he walked out of the room! Damn, Dog !!

So, I jumped out of bed and grabbed a shower, then let Gus out, and we made our rounds feeding all the animals, including the meat head. I started breakfast: Eggs, sausages, and toast! Aponi was up by then and dug in like a starving lion! Looking at her, my heart was killing me, then I thought, you better suck it up because I think she will be around a while; I knew she would want to go with me, and she couldn't wear the clothes she had on, so I grabbed some of Teresa's old jeans then under clothes and tee shirt! I showed her online how to put the underwear on, but she refused the bra, which is ok with me. I had to get a thicker tee shirt, so I got a Dr Hook concert tee shirt! It's a shirt we got back in the late eighties at one of their concerts! Baby makes her Blue jeans talk. That was a hit song back then, but that baby did make her Blue jeans talk, and did she ever!

We loaded up in the truck, and I got her buckled in, which I don't think she liked very much until I started down the highway doing seventy. Then her hands had a death grip on my dashboard and side console! She was so scared I had to slow down! She wasn't scared on the hoverbikes, so I wondered why now, but I guess it was something she had never seen before with traffic going both ways, We pulled into the distillery and walked into HR, and I retired and stopped my healthcare insurance! Healthcare in America is a scam all its own, as are the Car Insurance industry, the banking industry, taxes, and you get the drift! Sorry, I need to get refocused on the task at hand, like getting everything protected and pulling off some rescues without getting anyone killed, at least the good guys, anyway.

We pulled into a McDonald's and walked in. I ordered a couple of burgers, fries, and an Iced chocolate! Her eyes got big after the first taste, and I knew she was hooked while eating. I called Lee to see if he had any luck, and he gave me the name of the company where the corporate lawyer worked. After a quick Google search, I had the address, and we headed that way! Driving on I-65 was tough on Aponi, but downtown Louisville was about to put her into a frantic state! There was a small park next to the building we needed, so I walked her over and sat with her on a park bench! I smiled and hugged her until her heart slowed, then we walked in and asked to see Jennifer King and was shown to her office; after talking for about forty minutes, she raised a hand to stop me and said sir, the only reason I haven't called security was you are uncle Lees brother so now why are you here? I told her I wanted to hire her to start and preside over the company, and we only had a little over five hundred million but were expecting a few billion within a few months, and we would also need a Patent Attorney to start a few new Patents. I could see the disbelief in her eyes as she pushed her thick glasses up on her nose like Ernie does when he is nervous, so I opened my briefcase and took out my clear tablet, laid it on her desk then asked Alfred to show her a picture of the ship then she gasp when a brilliant picture showed up then I told Alfred to use that device to contact Lee, and after one ring Lee picked up and smiled and Said hay Shorty I'm so sorry to hear about your mom she was a good woman! Jennifer said thanks, Uncle Lee. I know she loved you, and I'm sad she pushed you away when she got sick. I know it hurt, but she thought she was protecting you from the pain. I believe she caused more pain than anything, anyway. It is good to see you. Please tell me your brother isn't taking one of your acid trips.

Lee laughed and said not that Stick in the Mud one good toke, and he would be lost for a month and laughed. I explained what happened and what we needed, then invited her to see the ship for herself! She said one of her friends that she went to Law school with was an excellent Patent Attorney, and she would invite her along and meet them the following day, so I wrote down the address and stuck out my hand. Then she pushed up her glasses and stood as she shook my hand. As she was standing, I thought she might need to duck at full height. She had to be six foot eight, maybe nine! A little shocked, I said Shorty, huh, she smiled and said I'm shorter than Anthony Davis and laughed as she pinched her forehead together to make one big eyebrow. I laughed and said the Unibrow.

We got home, let Gus out, and fed the livestock when my com device beeped. I turned the unit on and saw Chip with this beautiful blonde in the background. He told me he had three ready, and Alfred approved. Then, he asked me when I could come up! I asked Alfred if the hoverbikes could be seen or picked up by radar, and I had the answer before he could speak. No it wouldn't be picked up in stealth mode and showed me how to put in the directions but told me not to cross the sound barrier because that could and probably would be detected and tracked! Fifteen minutes later, we set our bikes down on the roof of Chip's apartment building, we knocked on his door, and that Beautiful hot blonde answered the door, shaking my hand and introducing herself as Air Force Captain Ali Shoptowh Friends call me Shitshow! Chip took over and introduced everyone there. First was a PJ or an Air Force Pararescue named TJ Running deer Myers, originally from the Navaho tribe. I chuckled at TJ, the PJ, and he smiled. Four months ago, he was a Master Sargent doing badass crap all over the world. They weren't just for rescue. They did a lot of special ops missions that no one knows about! Things I didn't even want to know about, so I shook his hand and said Much respect, bud, and thank you for everything you have done, and he just nodded! TJ was also single! The other guy was wearing Alligator Boots. Brandon Bates was a former Army ranger, Captain, so I asked why he got out. Then he reached over and knocked on his right leg with a metal pinging sound; apparently, he had the misfortune to parachute into an alligator nest while doing night training in the swamps of Florida! He said that was where he met TJ! He laughed. The gator took my leg, and I took his hide, tapping his boots, and TJ helped me load him up on the chopper. He then said he was married, but his wife left him when he lost his leg!

So, then I looked at Ali and asked so you want to be a part of this too when Chip spoke up, saying the reason Shitshow got her name was flying f-35s in combat because the more the chaos and the bigger the shitshow, the more in her element she becomes. She has to be a great leader because I would follow that gorgeous ass anywhere, I looked up as she smacked the back of his head while smiling the slid her hand in his and Daddy grinned, I could tell there was some deep affection already there then I asked her when she was due to resign her commission. She told me she was due to resign her commission in next month. She was thinking of flying commercial when this asshat told me about your situation so I'm hoping to sign on with you guys. I said I'm not sure of the pay right now but we will all share some of the profits!

Well, I guess we will take the two guys back with us and then ask if they have their gear. They both shook their heads, yes, so we loaded up after showing TJ how to fly the bike. Aponi climbed in behind me, and we took them to my place and put them in the guest rooms for the night! Gus did his inspection of them but, after a few scratches behind the ears, decided he liked them both.

CHAPTER NINETEEN:
BACK TO THE SHIP

We woke up late in the morning and fed everyone, and then Jennifer pulled in with her friend Christy, the Patent Attorney. She stood about five foot one with red hair and a well-built body. They both looked about Ernie's age twenty-three, maybe twenty-four. It is hard to tell these days anyway; we introduced them to TJ and Brandon, then headed for the sinkhole; as we were heading to the portal, I overheard Christy saying did you see that, Brandon? Damn, what a man Jennifer said he was ok but not my type. We walked through the portal and headed for my conference room. There, Greg and Ernie were going over schematics of something or another, looking up to say Hi then back to their task, so I had the two ladies sit down, but their eyes were everywhere like they were in a dream! Once I got their attention, I said We are willing to give you both point zero five percent of all profit from our patents and it will grow as we grow they both gave a sour expression and tried to negotiate for one percent, but Ernie spoke up and said he and Greg had six working models of the Fission reactors installed in their battle suits they were tested and ready to go then Christy broke in astonished did he say fission reactors and I said yes that would be one of our patents along with our clear tablets and a few more once her eyes went back to normal she looked at Jennifer and said I think zero point five percent will be more than enough! I was looking through the list of equipment we had on board and saw the mining tugs were autonomous, so I spoke with Alfred and had him send two of the four mining tugs out to the asteroid belt to start mining for precious metals. He said they were on their way. He also suggested sending the smelter to process the remaining ores from the mining tugs into sheets for later use. I told him that was a great idea because I wanted to build a few ships to protect this system from any other race who thinks they can pilfer what we have without any repercussions.

Alfred scanned TJ and Brandon for battle suits and get them an Armband ready, Alfred said yes, lord, then told Brandon that after he was scanned when he came on Board, the auto doc started printing, and his leg should be complete in six earth days. Then he said the armband was ready and to please follow him to the med bay. While they were gone, the girls met Greg and Ernie! When Ernie and Jennifer's eyes met, the way they both stared was funny. Then, after a full minute, they both pushed their eyeglasses up simultaneously! Jennifer grabbed Christy's arm and said now that's a man then walked over and reached for his hand! When he stood up at five foot seven and her six foot nine, you could see sparks flying. I just had to smile. All my boys looked to be falling in love, and after a thought, I was in the same boat. Then I remembered, oh shit, I forgot Gus, so I asked Aponi if she would like to go back with me when I dropped the girls off at their SUV. I also took a grave sled with all the gold and about half of the palladium, hoping that much weight wouldn't bust their shocks, and I gave them both com units and tablets. We sent them on their way with instructions on where to Start a company In Elizabethtown! I told her there were a few buildings that sat empty, including one old bank that was pretty large and could accommodate our needs, including a bank vault that would be needed for more precious metals. And If I weren't mistaken, there was vacant land behind it, and to buy as much land around it as possible! Jen then said she had to be careful when selling the metals to keep from saturating the market.

I then looked at Aponi, and I told her I wanted to take a bike up to Chip and leave it on the roof to use as needed, so we each jumped on one and headed northeast. On the way back, I called Chip and told him where we parked it and that it was in stealth mode and keep it under the speed of sound and let us know how everything was going with them and the recruitment. By then, we were drifting over the homestead, and I saw Lee's truck parked by the barn, so we landed then, fed the animals. Grabbed Gus, seeing Lee Walk toward me, I told him we really needed a building over the sinkhole and asked him to get with Alfred to put something up using the construction bots at night and that any design would do okay as long as it was secure and looked like it fit with the farm.

Seeing the pain on his face, I walked up, put an arm across his shoulders, and asked if he was ok, knowing personally the gut-wrenching pain he was going through with Jennifer's mom! Lee said he was saying goodbye and it was a little tougher then he imagined! Aponi came up and hugged him, and even Gus walked up, leaned against his leg, and licked his hand.

We were scanned and decontaminated ten minutes later as we walked through Med Bay. We walked up to the metal vessel and looked through the visual ports to see the progress of Brandon's new leg, which looked to be a third finished! On the way to the bridge, I stopped by Ernie's lab and found Greg, Ernie TJ, Brandon (Both in Battle Suits), and two new faces. A tall, dark, haired guy wearing a blue plaid shirt under his lab coat named Tim looked more like a lumberjack than a computer geek, but Ernie said he was a professor of computer science at MIT, and the rest of the introduction went in one ear and out the other! The only female of the group was a young, attractive dishwater blond named Gail, a professor at MIT and computer science, but had something to do with Nanotech! They had three helmets laid out and torn apart with chips, displays, and wiring harnesses in neat little rows! Ernie began with the helmets. They already had enhanced hearing and vision with inferred and night vision. The targeting was okay, but it depended on the operator's skill or lack thereof. Gail is working with Alfred to use the Nanites as an interface for pinpoint accuracy and enhance response time, but as of right now, that's at least a week away, and we are still taking input from the users on what they would like installed! It was their ass, after all.

Each suit has a rebreather, along with compressed air, to give at least thirty minutes of Air even in Vacuum. With the excess power from the reactor, we are experimenting with other enhancements. However, as of right now, we have eight suits ready to go!

Looking at Brandon and TJ, I could see the same itch I had in that they wanted some action.

CHAPTER TWENTY:
HILLBILLY ON MARS

I told Greg, Aponi, TJ, and Brandon to suit up and arm up because it was time to get something done. Then, Alfred explained that the mining habitats were running low on supplies, so it was a good time to shut them down. We then armed up with non-lethal weapons, mostly stun guns that would take a Charging rhino down and flashbangs, but I hoped it would go peacefully!

It took me a little bit to get my bearing in the suit because I kept bumping into the walls and chairs and tables and people! The only one smart enough to get out of my way was Gus! I looked down, scratched him behind the ear, and told him he would need to sit this one out. He looked at me like I lost my mind because I was scratching behind his ear instead of cussing him ! I wouldn't admit it but he was growing on me but I couldn't let him go because He was unprotected so asked Alfred if he could design Gus a workable suit. He said he anticipated the need and was working on one, but with dogs needing to pant to cool down, they would need a cooling system, and he had a few ideas, I asked Alfred to change the Destination on the ship's portal to one of the Mars habitats, and we walked through. It must have been a night cycle because all the miners were asleep in cots with one Guard keeping watch! He must have been having a conversation with Alfred because he jumped to attention as soon as he saw us and laid his weapon on the table in front! He tapped the other grey on the leg beside him to wake him up. Well, he turned out to be a she and was pregnant and didn't seem to be in a good mood! What the four hells do you want, burger? Then she saw us and tried to jump out of the cot. I held out a hand to stop her and told her my name, that I was now in command of all assets, and that I was shutting down all slave actions. Then she surprised me by saying Good, I hated slaving anyway! We woke all the slaves up, releasing them from their collars. They all seemed in pretty good shape, so I asked each one to push a gravsled full of ore to the cargo bay on the ship.

I approached the grays and asked what I would do with them! The male, I guess, was named Burger, and the female Tac. They both said we serve you, lord! Exasperated, I said well, let's get back to the ship, and Taco, make sure you report to the Auto doc for an exam! Yes, Lord! Ten minutes later, we popped out of the other portal On Mars, and this one turned into a firefight as soon as we hit the red dirt floor! They must have had more Loyalty to Lord Elos than the Ship because I was shot twice by a plasma rifle before I could get a good grasp of the room! All the slaves were hiding the greys as they fired on us! Shot after shot just bounced off our suits. It was almost funny, and they had to wonder why our shields weren't down when I yelled halt in my most command voice, but they didn't stop; TJ and I walked right up to both greys and took their rifles away.

So now we had forty slaves, four grays, and a shitpot load of ore that I had no idea what it was used for, so I asked Mr. Know it All, Alfred! He told me it was pretty rare. It had dual use, mainly used as an almost inexhaustible energy source for plasma. Also, mixed with other ores, it could be used for impenetrable armor. Seconds later, Ernie called asking for a sample! Alfred said it was called Cuxite and wasn't on our periodic table. So, I dropped a large sample off at his lab, noticing how excited he was acting, and asked, what's up? He looked at me and smiled. We were about to piss off the whole Oil Industry, giggling. He said Opec is going to love you! Why? I asked. Because our biggest Fission reactor can power New York, according to Alfred, pure Cuxite about this size can fuel it for a few years! Wow, I had to sit down. No, I had to Call Jennifer! Walking to my Office, I called her, sitting down as she picked up groggily, saying, " Yes, Mr Welch, how may I help you? I looked at my watch realizing it was five am there I said sorry for getting you up so early and call me Jack and she said call me Jen, please! First, I'm sorry for waking you, Jen. Something has come up, and we will need to grow quickly! Please hire a mining company that can and is willing to work off-world! Either hire them or buy them; it's up to you, but I'll need them within a week. Also, bump Christy's and yourself up to a full one percent! I had to take a deep breath. I doubt she went back to sleep! Too much was happening simultaneously, and I was being pulled in too many directions! Things were being put off, and people were suffering because of it! Time for a Family Meeting.

CHAPTER TWENTY-ONE: PRIORITIES

I called Chip and Ali for the meeting, and they walked in when I got started! I laid everything out that I needed help and that I wasn't capable of handling everything. Looking at Aponi, I said, darlin', you are in charge of our Indian assets! The ones that want to stay assign them Details! Find jobs they like and are willing to grow into, and if they don't mind mining, then hold them for Lee! The Braves that want to join our military send them to TJ or Brandon, or if they want to fly, send them to Captain Shoptowh. The ones that want to go home send them home; give them weapons of their timeline but nothing of any future timeline. Next, Lee, I want you to take over mining operations on Mars. After TJ and Brandon clear the moon Habitats, you will take over those operations. Also, get in touch with Jen about the mining company. Hell, what was I thinking? We could Fabricate our mining equipment, but we will need to expand those sites to accommodate those miners. However, that is your responsibility! He nodded his head and said yes, lord, with a grin! I looked at Chip. The Military is yours! TJ, I want you to recruit Special Ops Seals, More PJs, French Foreign Legion, and Russian Spetsnaz. If you can, Brandon, I want you to Recruit and train Ground Forces, which also includes worldwide, but make sure they are good people and have their heads on straight! I'll let you two plan and execute the rescue of the moon habitats. Also, Start planning The Philippine Assault, and I want to be in on that one myself! The Philippines is very dear to me! Looking at all the boys, I said that is where I met your mother After the meeting, I'll tell you about it!

Captain Shoptowh, I'm sorry, but I have a hard time looking at that Angelic face and calling you shitshow! You can call me Ali, Sir! I said thanks, and it's Jack! I want you to recruit and train our air and space forces. I want not just the flyers on board but also to build a fleet to protect our space sector! Chip that is also in your Wheel House!

Greg, how are our Mining tugs doing? Great, he Exclaimed! We have tons of Gold, Silver Palladium, and more than enough metal sheets to build two fleets. Smiling, I said good, but we need to add the correct mixture of Cuxite to fabricate armored hulls. Can you get with Chip and Alfred and start building my fleet now? Also, you are my second and overall Command! Sorry to lay all that on you, but I've seen your work and know you haven't even come close to hitting your stride. Ernie, I need you to keep doing what you are doing! Assist everyone you can, but I was hoping you could build the Sciences! Recruit the curious, innovative thinkers and use them to save the planet from ourselves, find ways to terraform Mars, and find other planets to settle! Also, get with Jen and Christy and make us some money because we will need a lot of cash. Also, let Jen know we will need Accountants upon accountants, and she and Cristy's percentage is going up! Ok, everyone not named Welch, get your lazy asses to work. I laughed. Aponi, you and Ali can stay behind.

CHAPTER TWENTY-TWO: MEETING THEIR MOM

1989 Clark AFB Pampanga

Province Philippines.

I had just finished changing out a Cypher lock on the control tower and was walking out of the Terminal when I noticed outside on a bench was an Air Force Captain Laid out on her side sleeping like a baby! I looked out across the sky and knew a big storm was about to roll in, so I walked over, admiring how Gorgeous she was.I tapped her on the shoulder, trying to wake her up! When she opened her eyes and I saw that beautiful smile, I knew I wanted to see her every day for the rest of my life, but I also knew I had to be careful because she was a Captain, and I was just a Staff Sergeant!

Mingling between Officers and Enlisted was strictly prohibited! I asked her if she wanted a ride to the BOQ (Bachelor Officers Quarters), and she said yes and got up! She had her Air Force Blues on, and she would make Hugh Heffner cry for his mama! I grabbed her duffle bag and started for the truck! Before we got halfway there, it started pouring rain, and we were both soaked! I pulled into the BOQ and she asked if I could wait while she checked in! Ten minutes later, she opened her door while I carried her duffle! I dropped it by her bed because it was just as soaked as we were! She walked into the bathroom, and I was trying to think of any excuse I could to stay close to her when she walked out with two towels. She dropped hers on the bed, took the other, and started drying my hair! I was mesmerized by those beautiful green eyes when she kissed me! As I was falling back on the bed, I kicked out my foot to close the door! We made love and talked, made love and talked! We snuck in and out of her room all weekend! Sunday night, I quietly pulled my Lock truck back into Our squadron's motor pool and left the paperwork for a week's leave! She told me she was heading to Australia for three weeks on leave and was taking Military hops to get there from Hicken AFB Hawaii. She was bumped off by an Army Colonel who married an Aussie lady that was giving birth in Sidney. I piped in Thank God For Aussie Babies! Two days later, we were secretly married out of Uniform by an Army priest with whom I played poker with only the cost of a Gallon Bottle of Jim Beam Black that I smuggled into the country! The Bourbon was well spent looking at my three boys, then Jen said Thank God for Aussie babies swatting Chip on the Butt and grinning!

All three boys came in for a hug, and with tears in my eyes, I asked each of them if they minded if Aponi was in my life. They all shook their heads no.

After the meeting, I grabbed a burger and fries and sat down to eat when Taco walked in and asked to talk, so I said, sure, have a seat, but with her long legs and big belly, she had to turn sideways! I said, whaz up when she asked what I was eating, and without thinking, I said burger and fries when she started crying. I didn't realize what was going on until I looked at the burger and started laughing; no, this is hamburger, not burger it took a while to calm her down when I gave her a fry she ate it, and her eyes got big, so I slid my fries over! I knew the greys were Omnivores and ate very little meat. While eating, I asked what she wanted to talk about, and she said she spoke to all the enocs, and they all wanted to stay and be as helpful as possible! Her clan was just one step above slaves in the order of things on their planet. They were not educated, but given the opportunity, she believed they could grow and be a real asset to the Ship! I smiled and asked when her baby was due, and she said Three! Most Enocs had Triplets, and she was due in a few days! So I ask her for a favor! Please get in touch with the Moon Habitats and ask them to Surrender and release the Slaves. Then I asked her for help processing both habitats and talking to those enocs to see if they were of the same mind! She said for another bowl of fries, she would grab them by the ears and bring them aboard herself! I laughed and ordered her more Fries and a Strawberry smoothie! Three hours later, TJ received word that both Moon Habitats were empty, and everyone had processed! I showered and laid down for a long overdue sleep! I was snoring within Seconds! I woke to look at my watch, thinking, holy molly, I must have slept twelve hours! I jumped up, showered again, and then went to slip my boots on, but my feet felt wet! GUSSSSSS I yelled as I caught a black tail run Out the door, and I could have sworn I heard a Laugh Damn Dog.

CHAPTER TWENTY-THREE:
PHILIPPINE RESCUE

After chasing the black furball all over the ship for a few hours, Alfred called me and told me Brandon's leg and Gus's suit were ready, so I called Brandon and told him it was ready and I would meet him in the med bay! I arrived a few minutes later, but he was already in the auto-doc! Alfred told me he would be there for at least twenty-two hours, so I headed to Ernie's lab. Gus was there decked out, and I must admit he looked sharp! The whole setup was slick. Gus would walk under the suit, tripping a sensor, and then the suit would come down and envelop him from the neck down. He walked out, then back under, then it came down, latched on to the suit, and it came off, and he walked out from under it, so I told everyone to turn around, walked up to the suit, and peed on it doing an about-face and walked out hearing Gus wine.

A week later, six of us are Flying over the Pacific, heading Toward the Island of Negros Occidental, Philippines, and landing in a cane field close to a plantation house owned By Alma Sanchez! Her son JJ and two nieces were kidnapped and are being used as Hostages! JJ was injured trying to protect his cousins, but they thought he would recover! I walked up to the compound and knocked on the Gate! A lady came out. She was short, had long black hair, and was very attractive. She had a beautiful smile. I could tell this smile was full of pain, worry, and hurt! Her son JJ was injured during the kidnapping trying to protect his two female cousins! She said she paid the six thousand tons of sugar cane that was Demanded, but her family hadn't been released, and she was about to round up her whole family and get them all back. I tried talking to her, but it was no use. Then Ken, one of TJ's new guys, started talking to her and calmed her down! He hugged her as we returned to our shuttle to wait for dark! While we waited, we geared up, including Gus! His suit was too small to have a fission reactor but was fitted with a high-capacity capacitor on each side of the suit. It had a charge indicator of three lights of red, three lights of yellow, and four lights of green, indicating a full charge, and it was full.

At eleven pm, we moved into position just outside the warehouse. With Inferred, we could see there were four of the Aliens in the middle of the warehouse and two in the offices! We waited for Alma's truck to show up so we could hide in the back and get a ride inside! We didn't have to wait but a few seconds when they rumbled in. Climbing in the back and covering ourselves with the plants, I felt us start to move. Then, I heard a horn and grinding as the doors opened. The truck pulled In, and we scrambled out. Taking down the aliens was pretty easy with just one shot! The extra power of the reactors in our pulse rifles making the difference! The two in the office came up, and Gus was on one. Before I could raise my rifle, Gus had him down with his throat in his mouth, and the guy was screaming like a wildcat! I guess they were guys. They looked almost human; except they were completely hairless. They had a light blue tint to their skin and a goatee! The other wall shot Gus three times before I put him down. I ran down and knelt beside Gus to make sure he was okay, then saw his indicator lights were down to two red lights left. I took a deep breath. I hadn't realized I was holding it, and I told him he would need to sit out for the rest of the mission! We double-zipped the last wall and walked into the portal. In an instant, we were on the floor of the Sulu Sea, and all hell broke loose! Plasma rounds were flying everywhere! I was overconfident in our shields and thought this firefight was in the bag when I got a call from Alfred that a probe from this cargo ship launched and was undetected until it hit lightspeed, but by then, it was too late. It couldn't be destroyed! Then I saw one Wall Soldier start shooting hostages. I quickly put him down when two more stood up to do the same. Brandon shot one, but the other raised his rifle to shoot two teenage girls when I saw a black flash, and the pulse lashed out toward its target! Gus couldn't get to the shooter, but he knew he could block those shots, and he did just that! The first shot dropped his shields, and the second and third tore into his body and vaporized his insides! One last whine, and he was gone! I leaned over him and cried like a baby! I couldn't stop crying. I had my helmet off. Aponi held me, and tears ran down her face! TJ took out the last Shooter, and with the firefight over, the families of the hostages poured in through the portal, trying desperately to find their loved ones! Looking up, I saw Alma holding the two girls Gus saved and her fourteen-year-old son, who held one Alien being in a headlock and wouldn't let go!

I finally pulled myself together with Aponi's help and asked Alfred to switch my call to the Philippine White House so I could call President Bong Bong Marcos!

An hour and ten minutes later, A chopper lands in the side parking lot, and President Marco's security team piles out to secure the location. A few minutes pass, and I shake his hand and tell him that the Philippines is the proud new owner of the world's first Interstellar Cargo Ship. Just then, a ship appeared fifty feet above the warehouse, still dripping water from the Sulu Sea, and you could see Burger waving like a loon out of the bridge window; the Ship was so large it was Blocking out the Sun!

Then, the real Hell broke loose! The Story broke worldwide just as I figured it would, and every Country wanted to contact us, which was good because we would need some help! According to one Wall prisoner, the probe carried a message about our attack on their ship, which constituted war in their eyes, and they would be coming to retrieve their ship and this planet as a prize!

CHAPTER TWENTY-FOUR:
GUS TO REST

I started to bury Gus beside Teresa in the family cemetery but thought better of it and took him to the meadow beside the river, where he tore that mohawk's butt up! Everyone was there, I guess, to support me! I think they were worried, especially the boys! They saw how rough Gus and I were to each other, but they knew how I felt about the big hardheaded slobber box hell he saved not only my ass but Greg's a few times. After all he did for me, I was unable to keep him safe. As everyone was walking away, I leaned over his grave and whispered Happy Hunting, you old fart. I'll miss you more than you could ever guess! Take care Of Teresa for me! I looked around then at the buffalo grazing in the fields across the river. I didn't know if Aponi would ever like to return to this timeline, but I would love to build a giant log cabin here. Lee walked up, putting his arm around me without talking. We walked slowly back to the toward Ship! Big brother is taking care of me again! I did notice a few red-haired pot plants along the way, but I just smiled. I wanted to check on the farm, so after walking through the portal, I noticed for the first time the LED lighting and tiled floors in the tunnel between the portals; taking a right, we headed to the sinkhole where it all started. The sinkhole was cleaned up with a wide ramp heading up toward the first floor! The construction bot and Lee did an excellent job on the two-story building! It looked like a typical barn and bunkhouse from the outside, but the inside was gorgeous, with over a dozen good-sized apartments overlooking an indoor Olympic-sized pool for guests.

We walked out in the midday sun with a nice breeze blowing! It was spring, with everything coming alive and turning green! I saw Koi riding Tersesa's Horse, Bella, down in the lower pasture and whistled to get his attention! Koi had taken over the farm operation, and I must admit it looked great! A couple of weeks prior, I received

eye of Torrox was first rotating around as a four-foot scale model, then the other three one at a time I told them all four were Antimonious and Could be AI-flown. But the AI's Downfall is Creativity, so they still needed crews, and we had crews to fit out two ships. We need Tacticians, we need Fighter pilots, and we need Mechanics and Engineers.

Our shipyards can produce Two destroyers every three Months, One Battleship every four months, and one Super Star Carrier every Six months, but it is all for naught if we can't crew and train them, so for that, we literally need Peace on Earth! Races and religions are working as one!" OTHERWISE" As I threw a Slave collar on the Podium, then walked out! I'm hoping my point was Made, But the UN was notorious for moving slowly and serving their own self-interest!

CHAPTER TWENTY-SIX:
ONE GOOD KISS

I was walking from the Mess Hall to the bridge, and as I walked past Ernie's Cabin, the door swooshed open! Curious, I looked in and saw Jen bent over Ernie, giving him a vivacious Kiss ! Smiling, I walked on, wishing Teresa was here to see her boys so happy, well, except Gus! I was still depressed about his loss, and I guess Aponi sensed that because she had spent more time with me wherever she could! I woke up each morning with her head on my shoulder! We still hadn't became intimate yet! I guess our Nanites are keeping our hormones in Check. Hell, it could just be my old age taking its toll. I wanted to give her more of a life! One morning I woke up with the hand of a beautiful woman on my member! Yeah, I know. Poor, poor me! The things a man has to endure, but I'll tell you this: life or no life, if it happens again, someone is in trouble!

After a six-hour shift on the bridge, I walked into my office to catch up on some paperwork when Ernie walked in! I leaned out and looked around him! He saw what I was doing and asked what? I said after seeing you vapor-locked this morning. I thought maybe you took Jen everywhere you went! Smiling, he said Ha Ha, very funny but then said that girl sure can kiss lost in thought for a second, and I had to bring him back. I asked him what he needed and told him to sit down! He brought up a 3D Hologram of what looked like a Pod!

He said he and the other two computer geeks (My Words, not his) had gotten together with Alfred and designed a Learning Pod to both teach crews their skills and also be used as a simulator to teach tactics and play war games! The Pods would learn as well as the students! Getting better after each use If a maneuver or tactic failed two files were created the first for failed tactics the second for failed tactic with possible successful variations and for successful maneuvers it was sent back and incorporated in the simulators and used against the trainees!

I told him great Bud, make as many as possible as fast as possible, that we had two crews, one Indian, the other Filipino, that needed training and we would send a couple to every major University on Earth.

After retrofitting the Hull with Armored Cuxite, beefing up the shields, and replacing the Fission reactors and offensive weapons on the Cargo Ship, the Philippine Government was more than happy to help us with our manpower problems! For some odd reason, China also pulled out of the South China Sea. Go figure! I suggested they rename the Ship Manny after Manny Pacquiao, A great Filipino Boxer because that ship packed a punch, but I think they went with Bituin Sa Umaga or Morning Star!

After lunch one day, I walked by one of our new training centers to catch a peak at some of the new students and saw JJ Sanchez climb out of the Pods! Surprised, I walked in and shook his hand. I looked at his epaulets to see the rank of First Lieutenant! I asked how he rose so fast at the age of Fourteen, and he told me he was now Fifteen and was taking College courses even before the kidnapping. His Commander walked up, a Full Bird Colonel, and said JJ had a unique Intellect in that he was like a sponge and soaked up Information with an insatiable desire, and he would go very far!

I think it was Hemmingway who said Write drunk and edit sober, but the way this is written, I bet you think that I wrote this drunk and edited drunk, you would be half right.

After the other Star Carrier came out of the Shipyard, Alfred cloned himself, but the Clone wasn't an exact copy. This one had a Female persona, so Greg called her Mama, and the ship he called

"VENGEANCE"! She was a beautiful ship, and she had teeth! The ship I acquired had Five pretty large Fission reactors: two for the engines, two for environmental, weapons, and shields, and one as a backup to be used where needed. The Vengeance had eight high-output fission reactors: Four just for the engines, one dedicated to shields, one to the environment, one to weapons, and one to be used where needed! Combined with a more formidable, sleeker Hull, she was faster and more powerful than any known vessel in any of the Memory banks in the Eye of Torrox, which reminds me I need to rename it.

I woke up in a lousy Mood! Still a bit depressed and pissed at myself for getting Gus killed after making a promise to Teresa. I was lying in bed, about to get up and shower, when Aponi walked in with a big box on a gravslead. I figured it had to be too heavy for her to carry! I sat up as she scooted the box off the sled onto the bed and opened the box lid when three black puppies jumped out, and two more waddled out! Five puppies that looked exactly the same, then I noticed they had small armbands with numbers from two to six. Then it hit me: Gus was number one, and these pups were cloned! I'm not sure how I felt about that. I always thought cloning could be very dangerous, so maybe I should have a talk with Alfred, but this toothpaste was already out of the tube. Better enjoy them while we can! I asked Alfred about the armbands and if the translators work for the Dogs! He said no, but it would help with their training.

I asked Aponi why there were so many; then she said I asked for Five: One for Greg, One for Chip, One for Ernie, and two for us. I said well, Greg is leaving tomorrow on his shakedown cruise so we should hand off number three before he heads out! Just then warning sirens started going off, and Alfred asked me to come to the bridge. I asked what was going on, and Alfred said three Wall battle cruisers just came into the System just outside the Kuiper

Belt, so me being the smart guy that I am, I asked where the hell is the Kuiper Belt then the answer came that it was close to Neptune! I think he really wanted to say something smart to follow up but was smart enough to reframe! I asked when they would reach us or at least Earth, and he said four hours before they were in range! I told everyone to rest for a couple of hours, eat, and then put their battle suits on and be ready for battle stations in three hours. I then put in a video call to Greg and the Captain of the Morning Star! I liked Captain John Zaponta the first time we met. He has a calm demeanor about him and a good sense of humor, usually at my expense, but I found that I could trust the man from the beginning.

I told John that the three cruisers were most likely coming for his ship, but he was free to leave at any time! He said he would like to tag along to see what she was capable of. I said glad to have you then to Greg, I told him since he hadn't had his Shakedown cruise yet that maybe he should follow but hang back a bit! Not sure I agreed, but the Morning Star took the lead as she got closer. I expected her to stop before we got into range, but she kept on, and that was when the Wall ships started pounding her with their pulse cannons. The Morningstar kicked into another gear, and she opened up with her cannons and railguns as she started to circle the three warships! I was hoping for a little action, but the Star was kicking ass. The first ship exploded in three large chunks, the second lost its engines, and the third put on the afterburners and jumped out of the system after the first shot took out its shields. They looked like old ships, so I didn't put too much into how easily they were put down, but I was very impressed with The Morning Star and her crew. She was a little larger than the Battle Cruisers, to put two down so quickly with minimum damage was eye-opening. But after being overconfident in our battle suits, I was trying to pump the breaks on being too optimistic.

CHAPTER TWENTY-SEVEN: PICKING UP THE PIECES

There weren't any life signs from the first Cruiser, but the second had quite a few, so I asked Brandon to send two squads of Marines over to take the ship and bring back prisoners. He looked at TJ and said, send hell, we want to go then I told them I wanted as many prisoners as possible and the ship intact.

Why build ships if you could refit them from someone else's nightmare? It seemed to work well with the old cargo ship! Tag along, my ass!

The Wall knew they had no place to go after their sister ship left them to their fate, but they were determined to take as many as possible with them! Their Captain, Unit Leader Daln started to fire on the shuttle, but if the shuttle had the same shields as that cargo ship, she knew that would be useless, so she logged into the self-destruct sequence and dropped the timer as low as it would go, which was one delnri (About 45 earth Seconds) and waited for the bump from the humans shuttle she knew was coming.

TJ put his armband up against the Airlock Control Module, and that gave Alfred an Avenue To gain Access to the Walls's Computer system. So, after just a few seconds, the Airlock Door opened, and the two squads rushed in, splitting up and clearing each room and cabin and department! One is heading to the bridge, and the other is to engineering! As Brandon and TJ walked onto the bridge, every Wall dropped their weapons on the Floor. TJ looked at the captain he thought was maybe a female but wasn't sure! It had big boobs but also was bald with a goatee, and It was smiling when a red light started flashing, and the grin got bigger! Alfred flashed a message not to worry, but the self-destruct sequence had just been initiated.

TJ shrugged his shoulders and said Yeah, nothing to worry about Alfred! Alfred countered that I could let it run down to one for dramatic effect if you wanted, but TJ just said no, now it is fine. He then stopped the countdown. The captain reached for her gun but was Stunned as her World went black. TJ thought for sure he Heard her say Crackheads! Damn, their Scouting program must be Top Notch.

Brandon asked why when TJ said she just Described the Whole Army Ranger Battalion laughing as he Dodged a Punch. There were Fourteen Walls left alive. After Debriefing, I walked down to the holding cells to see if I could get anything useful from the big-boobed captain. I walked in and sat in front of her, seeing her hands being handcuffed. I had the Indian guard remove them, and even though she gave me a deadly stare, I sat there waiting for her to talk first!

After a few long minutes, she squinted her eyes and said You stole our ship. I said two; we stole two of your ships now. Thanks! I thought she would come across the table, but she started laughing and said you would make a great Wall Politician because they steal us blind! I laughed myself and said we do have that in common! She leaned in close and said I hope you are ready for the Hell that's coming. She said three ships would get smashed in less than a delnri! I asked her name in a gruff voice, and she said Unit Leader Daln! I asked What was coming and when. Daln said her last count, The Wall Empire, had over one hundred War Ships, and right now, they were pissed and would be here within an Earth year. She must have taken pleasure in my facial expression because she smiled really big, and then she asked can you put me on your moon so I can watch Humanity die! I thought, Man, she must be a barrel of laughs at Parties. I said no, but there might be a few freaks shows on earth that might need a bearded lady, and walked out.

At first, I thought we might have a fighting chance of choosing quality over quantity, but that is a lot of quantity.

CHAPTER TWENTY-EIGHT:
THE WORRY BEGINS

The next ship off the docks was a Battleship and another clone AI from Alfred which again was another female-oriented AI I named Tab and then named the ship Freedom. Fitting her out with a crew was getting easier! After the UN meeting, we were flooded with people (mostly from Europe and Asia) wanting to protect the earth and their loved ones!

The United States was balking because they wanted to control! I guess all those sci-fi writers were right because it seemed every space opera, I have read said the same thing about our greedy government! The power they had was never enough.

If I lived through this upcoming battle, then maybe I would check into some of those asshats. A good House cleaning may be in Order.

The newly installed portals in Freedom and other ships made personnel assignments a lot easier. I moved her just outside Earth orbit while the captured Wall Ship and the Eye of Torrox were refitted with Cuxite armored plating, Adding more power and weapons to both. Yeah, I keep forgetting to rename her. Well, that is on the list—a very long list, but it's there.

I called a meeting to get everyone's input and find out where everyone was with their particular task.

I told everyone I wanted to play offense with the Walls! I want to take the Freedom, The Eye of Torrox and the new battle cruiser we took from the Wall and make an attack run through their system to slow them down. Alfred had a little problem breaking into their computer system and getting all the data we needed, including their complete system and defensive capabilities! We knew where to attack from and where to flee if needed. We knew what planets had their military bases and where the Shipyards were located. They were all for it!

I put in a video call with the four heads of state, The US, Russia, China, and the United Kingdom, and NATO's commander, and told them my plans and asked for their support! The United States and Russia were all for It and offered unlimited support, while the UK and NATO thought we would kick up a hornet's nest, and China had no comment, still pissed about the South China Sea, I guess My next video call was to President Marcos. After telling him about my plans, he said he liked the idea and offered support, but I could see relief on his face when I declined personnel support. I asked for a pallet of Philippine coffee with a laugh, and he said okay, and he would add a pallet of Balut. As my face turned white, he hung up, laughing. I guess he had the last laugh, and I was hoping he was kidding! Balut is a fertilized duck egg that was buried to stimulate development and then boiled or steamed! I tried one after a few too many beers before leaving the Philippines forty or so years ago, and now I can still taste it, Bluaaa!

After remembering the taste, I gargled Listerine a few times but still couldn't get it out of my system, I headed to the flight deck. I wanted to check out the new Fighters and Bombers. Ali Said they were badass, and they were! The fighter. It looked like if an F-15 and an F-35 had a badass baby, then that would be it. They had four fusion reactors themselves one four engines: one for weapons, one for environmental, and one to boost what needed boosting! The biggest reason it needed wings was to mount those four large pulse cannons, and the bombers were even worse. They were twice as large, taking two pilots and eight reactors with two pulse cannons and two mounted rail guns. Both models were AI-assisted, but pilot controlled! After salivating over them, I almost needed a cigarette.

CHAPTER TWENTY-NINE: MORE SHIPS THEN CREWS

I looked over the flight bay to see about five green flight suits hanging around talking, and one was a little shorter than the others. I thought that had to be JJ and walked over to where I saw Golden Oak leaves on his shoulders.

So, I ask What do you think of the Birds Major Sanchez, after returning his salute and pointing to both ships. Licking his lips, he said he was a Commander of a bomber and had only flown those, and with a big smile, he said, and they are frigging awesome I couldn't agree more.

I wanted to hop in one and buzz Earth a few times, but I had a mountain of paperwork to catch up on, so I headed back to my office. As I passed the mess hall, I looked in, and I saw Burger sitting, trying to feed three Enoc infants with Gus 2 and Gus 3 sitting under them, catching everything that hit the floor. I yelled. Two and Three, go find Aponi and pointed out the door toward Aponi's office. They both got up and pouted as they walked out, I almost said Damn Dogs but that thought made me laugh! While I was there, I grabbed Three slices of pizza and a large coffee and headed to my office! I don't know why I complain about the mound of paperwork. My thumbprint is my signature, so all I really have to do is read it and stick my thumb on the tablet. It's Jen who needs all the help! Last I checked, our patients were making literally billions a week, but even before Gus pulled me into that sinkhole, I didn't really care about money! As long as I was comfortable and the boys were doing Okay, then I was happy. Well, at that time, I was far from happy, but I was living! Thinking back, I'm Very happy with Aponi, but I still miss Teresa every day, and I doubt that hole will ever be filled completely, but Aponi is doing her darnedest! See, I'm trying to cut back on my cussing; shit, it's a work in progress. Who am I kidding?

We did get another Philippine Marine Company, and the United States loaned us one Seal team and a Company of Marines, but that was a drop in the bucket of what was needed! We were getting Fighter and Bomber pilots, and after a few weeks in the Learning/Simulators, they were flying them like they were born in them. Plus, the AI assistants had kept a few collisions from happening, but we had more ships than crews! Our inventory had three Destroyers and two cruisers waiting on crews! Chip and Ali were using partial crews for their shakedown cruises, and that included all of the greys. Finding good people is crucial! Taco turned out to be a very important leader for us, both for the greys and our human crews. She had a no-nonsense approach to everything, the exact opposite of burger, we all knew, who wore the battle suit in that family!

After breakfast one morning, I pinged Greg and asked him to come to my office! He walked, sat down, and opened his tablet, knowing full well I was about to ask him a ton of questions! I started with Fabricators. We were to send one large Fabricator to each continent on Earth, along with a few hundred tons of Cuxite and a few hundred tons of iron oxide, to knock out as many battle suits as possible!

I was pretty sure this was going to be a knockdown-dragout ground war before it was all over with. The Fabricators themselves were dual-purpose, one producing the Cuxite armored Suits with the Fission Reactors and the other Producing the helmet as well as the visor, software, and components! We estimated each Fabricator could produce a little over eleven hundred Suits a day as long as each of the elements needed were fed properly.

CHAPTER THIRTY:
HEAD EM UP

I wanted to spend some time with Aponi before I Left! She didn't know, but I was planning on keeping her here planet side, so I grabbed my backpack, my shotgun, a couple of fishing rods, and my beautiful girlfriend, then headed to the 1700's.

I'm not sure how time then corresponded to Time now, but I wanted to spend the weekend with her and soak up as much of her as I could, so after setting up camp and putting a couple of lines in the river, I pulled my Lady in for a deep romantic kiss! I looked into those green eyes and, as Sincerely as possible, said, "Aponi, my Darling Lady, I love you, and I want to spend the rest of my life holding you, kissing you, and Making Love to you. Then I went down on one knee, shaking as I pulled a ring out of My pocket; nervously almost dropping it, I asked Sweetheart, Will You Marry Me? My heart was pounding in my chest because I had no idea what she would say! She stood there, and then a tear slid down her gorgeous face. She then pulled me up, hugged me, and then backed away about three feet, picked up a rock, and put it in my hand! Looking at it, I asked what do I need to do with it?

If a Brave wants to marry a Maiden, he throws a stone at her feet. She then picks it up, and if she walks away, then the matter is closed, and he must move from the village, but if she picks it up and throws it back, then the brave has to leave and bring presents to the maiden's family. I smiled and cast my stone, trying not to hit her feet. Scared, she would turn and walk away, and she did! Aponi picked up the stone and turned to walk away. My heart sank, and I almost dropped to my knees, then she ran and jumped into my arms, dropping the stone at my feet! We both laughed and cried at the same time! She said Jack, you beautiful, silly white man, I love you too, and I want to live in those arms! You may not have known it, but you have been my man for a long time now, and you are not leaving me behind on this next mission!

Why am I always a step behind everyone else? I wondered as I was lost in wonderful lovemaking! I could have sworn our souls were intertwined! Every touch, every kiss, every nibble was branded in my psyche! We made love for hours, then took a swim in the river and made love there! I finally fell asleep with Aponi's head on my shoulder at about Three Am, and I dreamed of Teresa overlooking us as we made love. She said it is ok, my dearest. We both love you, so live a Beautiful Life.

That was the first time in years that I went to sleep astoundingly happy and woke up astoundingly happy! We had everything to live for and, with our nanites, would live for a few hundred years together. I just needed to make sure it wasn't with a slave collar on our necks.

CHAPTER THIRTY-ONE: LEAVING THE SYSTEM

It had now been over three months since we took the last wall cruiser named Destiny; it had been rebuilt using the Cuxite armor with our engines, then replacing their five old Fission reactors with eight and upgrading their weapons and shields. She was still ugly, but she was also an ass-kicker, and she was Chips New Ship. I asked him why he chose that ship for his Headquarters instead of one of the new Destroyers, and he looked at Ali and said I already have a beautiful lady in my life; I don't need another! I smiled as I walked out of his stateroom before it got too mushy and hot.

Lee and Koi took command of the new Destroyer Named The Eagle! Which also had a Female AI named Brenda! I asked Alfred why all the Female AIs when he snickered and said you Humans aren't the only ones that like to play with ladies. I started to say something smart about thinking he was Gay, but Common sense finally kicked in, and I walked out whistling.

I was taking the newly named Super Carrier, the Choctaw, which is formally known as the Eye of Torrox. Yes, Scratch one more off the ever-expanding list. We had a Company of Philippine Marines, a Seal Team, and A full complement of the New Fighters and Bombers! The Eagle was taking a Company of US Marines, and I was hoping Lee didn't bring along his Grow room even though I know he brought his peace pipe because it always hangs behind his desk (decoration, my ass) The Freedom would be left behind much to my disappointment. We were ready to go! Everyone Spent hours upon hours in the simulators trying to learn as much as possible about Fighting our Ships Individually and as a team! Our War Planning is all laid out we were ready or so I thought The Whole Family ported over to Vengeance to say goodbye to Rob, Opa, and Earnie, where Earie showed me something cool! He held a clear dome that was about a foot high and a foot circle! He said he and a Chemical Engineer, a Civil Engineer, and a Metallurgist Came up with a plan to build a city on the Mars plains with it! It worked like a 3D printer, but instead of concrete, it was printing a Cuxite Dome. In the last month, they had built a gigantic airlock large enough to bring a Battleship through and printed close to four hundred square miles around the Cuxite mine and will butt up next to Arsia Mons, a ten-mile-high Volcano near the Equator, where they plan on building an underground city into the Volcano! The Dome is forty percent complete and should be finished by the time we are back! Apparently, Aluminum added with the Cuxite and Hematite, an Iron ore, also blocked both galactic cosmic rays and solar energy particles, so with the right soil Mixtures, farming could be entirely possible.

I said I look forward to seeing it when I get back in a few months! I thanked everyone I could and hugged more than I should! Hay I was Emotional!

Three hours later, Our FTL drives kicked in, and we were on our way! Hell, or High Water!

CHAPTER THIRTY-TWO:
KICKING THE HORNET'S NEST

We were about ten hours from dropping out of FTL, so I called all of our brass over for one more briefing to cement our plans and to make sure all three ships were combat-effective! Something was off.

I just had a nagging bad feeling I was missing something important.

I started to call the Mission off, but the Determination on everyone's face made me suck it up and go ahead with our Hit and Run plans.

Chad, our new Pilot, Said Dropping out of FTL in Ten seconds! I said Shields up and at one Hundred Percent! Ready all weapons! Chad, I want to start our Attack run on their Second planet's First moon at the Military Base, then head for their Shipyard around the Third Planet, then as many ships as we can hit on our way out! Yes, sir, that was the reply; I looked at TJ on the Weapons. He winked and said all railguns and pulse Cannons were ready and waiting on targets. We also had a few old ICBM Missiles to throw at them, but so far, they were not needed.

After the run, the military base was completely demolished! The shipyard was a different story; they had their defense platforms up and ready. I'm glad we only needed one pass over the Shipyard because that platform was kicking our ass! I got a notice from Alfred that our shields were down to sixty-six percent! I told Alfred to scan those Platforms because I wanted those around Earth and Mars. Yes, Lord was his answer. So, I guess we are back to Lord now?

After the shipyard, we annihilated four ships, and then, out of nowhere, a large Asteroid came flying at us. Only Chad's reaction time saved us. Lee and the Eagle had a little more time to react, and it sailed harmlessly past them, but Chip's ship wasn't so lucky because they were right on the Eagle's ass. The asteroid hit Midship, raking down the ship, taking out their number two Engine, damaging the first, and taking the shields completely offline! My heart went cold when Alfred told me about the damage to Destiny! The Wall must have seen the blood in the water because almost every ship in the system was heading for Chip's ship! I asked Alfred how many wall ships were in the system when we arrived. Eighty-seven was his answer, and then I wondered aloud where the rest of their fleet was when everyone's face dropped at the same time! I saw Ali, My Second in command, start to run off the bridge when she hollered. I'm taking two fighters and Two bombers to help Chip! Please get home as fast as you can so we have somewhere to go home, too! I yelled GO, then called Lee and told him what was going on with Earth then told him to get everyone off Destiny as fast as possible and get out of dodge pronto, and then after enough separation, took the Chocktaw into FTL as fast as I could get her home!

CHAPTER THIRTY-THREE:
THE WALL EMPIRE

The Eagle was taking out ships as fast as he could while Chip was sending every able-bodied man he could through the portal, resigning himself to be the last through when he heard the hatch blow. Then he knew he was being boarded. There were twelve men left to go through the portal. When the grenade landed at his feet, he then woke up two days later with a collar around his neck strapped to a med bed! He looked around to see Brandon and six others, including Major JJ Sanchez, with his second collar around his neck in his very short life!

Lee waited by the portal for Chip and the rest of the Crew of the Destiny, where he heard Gunfire and grenades going off in the other Ship. Then one fell at his feet as he dived for cover telling Brenda to shut the Portal!

Lee wanted to stay to get Chip and the others out of there but he wasn't even sure Chip was still alive! The eagle was taking a pounding with his Shields down to twenty percent. He ordered her to FTL Ali took the four small ships into complete Chaos but they didn't call her Shitshow for nothing she and the other pilots used every trick they could! They used speed and maneuverability to cause as much havoc and damage as they possibly could, but eventually, they, too, were swatted from space.

Chip cried when JJ told him Ali was lost! The last he saw; her ship was on fire and heading on a collision course with a destroyed Wall Cruiser! It had been three weeks since they were captured! Now shirtless, working on a lifeless moon, he looked up and said, "Dad will come." As an electric whip slashed across his back, he glared at the Wall guard and said, I can't frigging wait!

CHAPTER THIRTY-FOUR:
FIVE WATCHING ROME BURN

When we came out of FTL, Wall Dropships Were Disparaging Troops from Troop carriers all over Earth. Alfred said Lord The Vengeance and Freedom were in a battle around Mars with over thirty-eight cruisers and three Wall Battleships! Both our ships were giving as much or more than they were getting! As soon as the shields would drop a little then the fabricators would spit out a few new emitters to bring them right back to one hundred percent! It took two hours for us to get there, but we turned the tide a little quicker than they could on their own, and soon, one Wall battleship and three cruisers surrendered! We had Air Superiority now, so retaking Earth shouldn't be a big problem, but as I watched cities burn, I stood there with tears in my eyes, asking myself, What Have I Done?

Ali Scooted up to the very edge of the ledge overlooking the slave camp. With her Tuck one of the Choctaw Pilots also peeked over while holding his bow and quiver. Her blood began to boil when she saw the guard lash out with the whip across her man's back and almost shot him before she had gotten control of herself!

Tuck laid a hand on her arm and said Soon Boss! Soon we will get them out!

End of Book one

www.ingramcontent.com/pod-product-compliance
Lightning Source LLC
Chambersburg PA
CBHW040154160726
48006CB00014B/1749